OTHER YEARLING BOOKS YOU WILL ENJOY:

THE GHOSTS OF COUGAR ISLAND

Peggy Parish
Illustrated by Deborah Chebrian

A YEARLING BOOK

Published by
Dell Publishing Co., Inc.
1 Dag Hammarskjold Plaza
New York, New York 10017

For Allison Epps with love

Yearling ® TM 913705, Dell Publishing Co., Inc.

ISBN: 0-440-42872-6

Printed in the United States of America

June 1986

10 9 8 7 6 5

CW

Contents

·1·

Almost Over

"Gee, the summer is almost over," said Jed.

"It seems like only last week that we came to Pirate Island," said Liza.

"It seems more like forever to me," said Bill. "Think of all the things that have happened."

"It has been our best summer yet!" said Liza.

"We say that every summer," said Jed, "Remember the fun we had last summer on the farm with Gran and Grandpa?"

"Yeah," said Bill, "we sure surprised Grandpa when we solved his grandfather's puzzle and found the treasure."

The children talked about this adventure. They had spent the previous summer on their grandparents' farm. Grandpa had told them a story about his grandfather who had to go off to war. This made his children very unhappy. To cheer them up, Grandfather left them a puzzle to solve. The first clue to the puzzle was accidentally destroyed. Grandfather was killed in the war, so the puzzle had never been solved. Each generation of children had tried unsuccessfully to solve it. It was by accident that Liza, Bill, and Jed found the first clue. After that, nothing could stop them from searching until they found the key to the treasure.

"Then Gran told us about the disappearing garbage," said Liza.

"We got into plenty of trouble trying to solve that one," said Jed.

"And had some scares too," said Bill.

In their second adventure, *Clues in the Woods*, some neighboring children asked Gran to save her table scraps for their kittens. Gran would leave the scraps outside each night for the children to pick up. One morning Gran saw the children leaving empty-handed. She called them to find out why. They thought she had forgotten to leave the scraps and didn't want to bother her. Gran began putting the scraps inside the can for them. But the scraps still disappeared. Gran was completely puzzled and told the story to Liza, Bill, and Jed. They eagerly started working on this mystery. During the course of following the clues they found in the woods, they ran into exciting and sometimes scary adventures.

"That was great fun," said Liza.

"Hey," said Bill, "where are we going?"

"I want to explore this end of the island again," said Jed. "Does anybody have a better idea?"

"Not me," said Bill, "I don't even know how we got here!"

"I'll explain it to you, twin brother," said Liza. "Jed walked out of the back door and we followed."

"That sounds like us," said Bill. "We just follow the leader. Hey, Jed, how does it feel to be the leader?"

"Oh, cut it out, Bill," said Jed.

"Well, you do have the best ideas," said Liza.

"I do not," said Jed, "You and Bill come up with some dillies, especially Bill."

"That's me," said Bill, "Dilly, dilly Billy, at your service."

Liza and Jed laughed as Bill began clowning around.

"Ta-ta-de-dum, end of the island, here we come," chanted Bill. Liza and Jed fell in behind him and began chanting too.

After a while Bill stopped. He said, "Boy, that made me thirsty. I'll race you to the spring."

Bill took off running. Liza and Jed raced after him.

"Beat you!" yelled Bill.

"Of course you did," said Jed. "You had a head start."

"Just a short drink, please, Bill," said Liza. "I'm really thirsty."

Bill went right on drinking from the spring.

"Please, Bill!" said Liza.

Bill pretended not to hear.

"Okay," said Liza. "You asked for it."

She pushed Bill's head into the water. Bill came up sputtering.

"Cut that out!" he said. He began drinking again.

"All right, Bill," said Liza. "You're going to get it."

Bill looked up and grinned. He said, "Did you want a drink, Liza?"

Liza was furious. She kicked Bill in the seat of the pants. He toppled into the spring. Now Bill was furious. He scrambled out and started for Liza.

"Dirty fighter!" he yelled. "Put your mitts up."

"All right, you two!" shouted Jed. "Go ahead and kill each other. I'm through with you."

Jed walked off. Liza and Bill looked at each other. It was unusual for Jed to get so angry.

"I'm sorry," said Liza.

"So am I," said Bill. "Truce?"

"Truce," said Liza. They shook hands.

"Think we'll ever learn to control our tempers?" asked Bill.

"I doubt it," said Liza. "Let's catch up with Jed."

"Hey, aren't you forgetting something?" asked Bill. Liza looked puzzled.

"That drink you wanted so badly that you almost drowned me," said Bill.

They both began to laugh. Liza got her drink, then they started after Jed.

"Hey, Jed, wait up," called Bill.

"We have a truce," said Liza.

"For how long?" asked Jed. Bill and Liza looked at each other.

"Maybe for the rest of the day," said Bill.

"That would be a record," said Jed.

"Miracles do happen," said Liza.

"Ta-ta-de-dum, end of the island, here we come," shouted Bill. "Isn't that where we left off before the battle started?"

"Close enough," said Jed, grinning at Bill.

·2·

Jelly Bean's
Discovery

The children walked along in silence, each deep in thought. Liza, Bill, and Jed were spending the summer with their grandparents on Pirate Island. The Robertses had owned a home there for several generations, but this was the children's first visit. Their grandparents usually came for the month of December when the caretaker and his wife were away. But the caretaker had died, and his wife had gone to live with her daughter. So Gran and Grandpa had decided to spend the summer, and they had invited Liza, Bill, and Jed to stay with them.

Many years before, when Grandpa was just a boy, his older

brother had made up a treasure hunt for Grandpa and his sister. He had hidden some things belonging to different members of the family on the island. He planned to have them find the treasure the following summer. But things had not worked out as he planned. It was many years before the family returned to the island. The brother left home to go to work. Before he left, he gave them the first clue. Later he was killed in an accident. The treasure hunt had never taken place.

Just before coming to the island, Grandpa had told the children the story and given them the first clue. As soon as they got to the island Liza, Bill, and Jed had set out to find the treasure. It was a hard puzzle, but they finally solved it.

While they were having their first Pirate Island adventure the children were told to stay out of the way of an islander called Hermit Dan. Hermit Dan wasn't a true hermit, but he had little to do with people. He seemed to dislike children especially. Hermit Dan had grown up on Pirate Island. He had been a perfectly nice person and well liked by the islanders. Then something had happened that made him change. The islanders didn't know what. Hermit Dan left the island and was gone for many years. He returned, built himself a shack, and went about his own business.

But Hermit Dan was also a thoughtful man. He had a large vegetable garden and kept the islanders supplied with vegetables. He never gave the vegetables to the people but left them on their steps for them to find. Hermit Dan was a man of mystery, and for Liza, Bill, and Jed, *mystery* was a magic word. They were determined to solve the mystery of Hermit Dan. It had turned out to be an exciting and rewarding adventure.

Now the children had no goal other than to have fun.

"Yap, yap, yap!" A sharp bark broke the silence.

"Jelly Bean!" said Liza. "I thought he was with Gran."

"I guess he had plans of his own," said Bill. "Come on, Jelly Bean, we're over here."

"Yap, yap, yap."

"He sounds close by, but I don't see him," said Jed.

"He's up to something," said Liza. "I know that bark."

"I sure hope it's not another skunk," said Jed.

"Yuck," said Bill. "That's one experience I don't want to repeat."

"I'll find him," said Liza. She started toward the yapping.

"He may be stuck again," said Jed. "Remember when he landed in the top of a bush?"

Bill laughed and said, "Jelly Bean has given us lots of laughs. Let's help Liza look for him."

"Jelly Bean, where are you?" called Liza.

"Yap, yap, yap," answered Jelly Bean.

"Well, come on out," said Liza. "I can't get through those bushes."

But Jelly Bean continued to yap.

"Oh, all right, I'll try," said Liza. She began to push into the thick brush. "The things I do for you. This had better be worth it."

Jelly Bean continued to yap. Liza continued to push her way through the brush. Suddenly she broke through into an open space. Before her lay a thick carpet of green moss.

"Oh," she said. "It's like a fairyland. Jed and Bill have to see this."

Jelly Bean yapped louder. Liza looked to see what he was doing. She began to laugh.

"Jelly Bean!" she said. "You're going to scare that little frog to death."

Jelly Bean stopped yapping. He and the frog stared at each other.

"Jed! Bill!" yelled Liza. "Come quickly!"

"What's wrong?" yelled Bill. "Did something happen to Jelly Bean?"

"No," yelled Liza. "Come and see what he found."

"I can't even see you," said Bill. "How do we get there?"

"Just push through the bushes," yelled Liza. "Follow my voice."

"Ouch!" yelled Bill. "Why didn't I wear long pants?"

"We didn't expect this," said Jed. They pushed on and broke into the opening.

"Wow!" said Jed. "How did we ever miss this place?"

"Easily," said Bill, rubbing his scratches.

Liza took off her shoes. She dug her toes into the moss.

"It feels just like velvet!" she said.

"Yap, yap, yap," went Jelly Bean. The frog hopped, and

Jelly Bean hopped. Then the frog hopped into the water. Jelly Bean yapped one last time as the frog disappeared.

Liza, Bill, and Jed sat on the soft moss and looked out over the water. Not far away was another island. It looked to be about the size of Pirate Island, but no one lived on it.

"I sure would like to explore that island," said Jed.

"I was thinking the same thing," said Liza. "It looks so close."

"Think we could swim across?" asked Bill.

"Bill!" said Liza. "You know Gran would have kittens if we tried that!"

"Now that I would like to see," said Bill.

"What?" asked Jed.

"Gran'll have kittens," said Bill.

"You know what I mean!" said Liza.

"Okay, okay," said Bill. "But couldn't we swim it if we wore life jackets?"

"I think that's too risky," said Jed. "We need a boat."

"Fat chance we have of getting that," said Bill.

"How deep do you think the water is?" asked Liza.

"What a dumb question!" said Bill. "How would we know that?"

"Cool it, Bill," said Jed. "Liza looks as if she has an idea."

"Okay, twin sister," said Bill. "Out with it."

"A raft," said Liza. "Couldn't we build a raft? That would be safe."

· 11 ·

"Good idea!" said Jed. "That shouldn't be too hard."

"Think some more," said Bill. "We would need boards to build a raft. Where would we get the money to buy them?"

"No problem," said Jed.

"Think, Bill," said Liza.

"Just do me one favor," said Bill.

"What?" asked Jed.

"Please tell me what I'm supposed to think about," said Bill. Liza and Jed laughed.

"You really are impossible," said Liza.

"I'll give you a clue," said Jed. "The big shed by the barn."

"Get it?" asked Liza.

"Shhh," said Bill. "The old brain is at work."

Bill put on his thinking act. Liza and Jed laughed again. Finally Bill said, "Aha, I've got it! The shed is filled with scrap boards. We can use them to build a raft."

"Hurray!" shouted Liza and Jed.

"Let's go," said Bill.

"Hold it a minute, Bill," said Jed. "Liza, why were you asking about the depth of the water?"

"I thought if it wasn't too deep," said Liza, "that it would be easier to pole a raft rather than paddle."

"You're right," said Jed. "Maybe we can find out the depth from Grandpa. He stores up facts like that."

"I know something else too," said Bill.

"I know what you're going to say," said Liza.

"Oh, yeah?" said Bill. "What?"

"That you're hungry," said Liza.

"Come to think of it," said Bill, "I am, but that isn't what I know."

"So are you going to tell us," said Jed, "or do we play Twenty Questions?"

"Be glad to tell you," said Bill. "I smell adventure."

Liza and Jed grinned. Jed said, "So do we!"

·3·

Waiting for Grandpa

As the children walked home Liza said, "Do you really think we'll find another mystery to solve?"

"I don't see why not," said Jed. "Dad and Grandpa said Pirate Island was filled with mysteries."

"But first things first," said Bill.

"What do you mean?" asked Liza.

"I mean, it's lunchtime," said Bill, "and I'm really hungry."

"Let's go," said Jed. The children broke into a run. They didn't stop until they reached the back door.

"There you are," said Gran. "I was hoping you would come soon. Lunch is ready."

"That's what my stomach told me," said Bill.

"Wash up and come to the table," said Gran. "Give Grandpa a call."

Soon they were all enjoying lunch.

"Did you have a good morning?" asked Grandpa.

"We sure did," said Jed.

"Oh, Grandpa," said Liza. "We found the prettiest place hidden away. It's all velvety moss."

"My dreaming place," said Grandpa softly.

"What did you say?" asked Bill.

"That's my dreaming place," said Grandpa. "How did you happen to find it?"

"By accident," said Liza. She told him about Jelly Bean and the frog.

"I found it by accident too," said Grandpa. "I guess I was about your age at the time. It was my secret. I used to spend hours there. Sometimes I would take a picnic lunch and a book. Other times I would just look out over the water and dream. I don't think anybody else knew about it."

"It's great," said Bill. "I'm glad Jelly Bean helped us find it."

"Grandpa," said Jed, "from there the next island looks so close."

"Yes," said Grandpa, "that is the closest point between the islands."

"Is the water very deep there?" asked Liza.

"No," said Grandpa. "Probably at one time the two islands were connected."

"It looks like a nice island," said Jed. "Why doesn't anyone live there?"

Grandpa began to laugh. He said, "See, Gran, I told you it would happen before the summer was over."

"What would happen?" asked Liza.

"That you would get curious about Cougar Island."

"Cougar Island!" said Bill. "Are there really cougars there?"

"Not the four-legged kind," said Gran. "A family by the name of Cougar owned that island."

"Did they ever live there?" asked Jed.

"Oh, yes," said Grandpa. "Many generations of Cougars were born and grew up there. The last one died when I was a boy."

"Come on, Grandpa!" said Bill. "I know you have a story to tell. Stop holding us in suspense."

Gran laughed and said, "Your grandchildren really know you."

"We're waiting, Grandpa," said Liza. Grandpa looked at his watch.

"You're going to have to wait some more," he said. "I promised Captain Ned I would check out a house with him."

"Grandpa!" said Bill.

"Sorry," said Grandpa. "The story will keep until I get back."

He left quickly.

"Isn't that just like Grandpa," said Liza. "We're all excited, and he tells us we have to wait."

"A promise is a promise," said Gran. "Find something to do and the time will pass quickly."

"Couldn't you tell us the story, Gran?" asked Bill.

"No way!" said Gran. "You know what your Grandpa would say."

"Don't steal my thunder!" yelled the children.

"Exactly," said Gran. "Besides, I promised Jenny Hawkins I would help her make raspberry jam."

"Mmm," said Bill. "Will you bring home a sample?"

"That you can count on," said Gran. "You know Jenny."

·4·

Interrupted
Plans

"Gran's right," said Jed. "Time will pass faster if we're busy."

"Let's start the raft!" said Bill. "That will keep us busy."

"I'll get a pencil and paper," said Liza.

"For what?" asked Bill.

"Oh, Bill!" said Liza. "We have to plan the raft."

"Phooey," said Bill. "Plan, plan, plan. Why can't we just build it?"

"Liza's right," said Jed. "We have to figure out the size so we know what materials to look for."

"Oh, all right," said Bill. Soon the three were busily making suggestions.

"Okay," said Jed, "I think we know what to look for now. Keep your fingers crossed that we can find enough boards the right size."

"What about poles?" asked Bill. "Nobody mentioned them."

"We'll have to cut those ourselves," said Jed.

"Chop down trees?" said Bill.

"There are plenty of saplings. They shouldn't be too hard to cut," said Jed.

"Maybe Grandpa will help us," said Liza. "He has a chain saw."

"Good idea," said Bill. "It would take us forever."

"Everybody ready?" asked Jed.

"Let's go," said Liza.

The three dashed out to the shed by the barn.

"Boy, with all this stuff surely we can find everything," said Bill. Jed looked all around. Finally he saw a board he wanted.

"Hey, Bill," he said. "Give me a hand."

Bill hid his hands behind his back. He said, "No! I can't give you a hand. I need both hands. They're good hands. I love my hands."

Liza and Jed groaned.

"How did I ever get you for a brother?" asked Liza.

"Just luck," said Bill.

"Cut it out and help me get this board," said Jed. Bill

rushed over and helped Jed. Soon they had the board out of the shed.

"Well, what do you think?" asked Jed.

"It looks the right length to me," said Liza.

"Okay," said Jed. "Let's see how many we can find the same length. We'll use this one to measure by."

The children pulled board after board from the pile. If it was close to the right length, they laid it beside the first. The others were put back in the shed.

"Gosh," said Bill. "That looks like enough."

Jed looked at them and said, "Let's sit on them. We can tell better that way. We don't want it too big to handle, but we sure don't want it too small."

The children found places on the boards.

"What do you think?" asked Bill.

"It should be a little larger," said Liza.

"Yeah," said Bill. "Maybe another board or two."

Two more boards were quickly found. The children tried out the size again.

"Just right," said Bill. "Now what?"

"We need three cross ties to nail them to," said Jed. "I know there are some here, but where?"

The children had to do some searching. Finally Liza spotted them.

"Back in the corner," she called. "I'll get the first one."

"They're heavy," said Jed. "I'll help you."

Liza was already pulling one out with all her might. Suddenly she dropped it and screamed.

"Liza, are you hurt?" asked Bill.

Liza shook her head and pointed.

"A giant rat!" yelled Jed.

"It ran across my foot," said Liza. "I'm not staying here!"

She ran out of the shed. For once the boys did not make fun of her. They wanted nothing to do with rats, either.

"Liza, what's wrong?" called Grandpa. He came running to the shed.

"Grandpa!" said Bill. "You're home."

"I know that," said Grandpa. "Liza, what's wrong?"

"A big rat ran across my foot," said Liza. She threw her arms around Grandpa.

"A rat!" said Grandpa. "It must have come over on one of the boats. I'll take care of that. We don't need rats on this island."

"How will you get rid of it?" asked Jed.

"With rat poison," said Grandpa. "I'll call and have some sent over. In the meantime you all stay out of that shed."

"Don't worry about that," said Liza. "That rat was huge."

"I'll ask them to send the poison over on the four o'clock boat. If I put it out tonight, tomorrow there should be a dead rat," said Grandpa.

"Jelly Bean!" said Liza. "What if he gets the poison?"

"Don't worry," said Grandpa. "I'll shut the door. He won't get in."

The children followed Grandpa to the house.

One end of Pirate Island was mostly wooded. The permanent residents, or islanders as they called themselves, lived here. The other end of the island was a resort. During the vacation season it was filled with what the islanders called summer people. The islanders had little to do with the summer people and made it clear that they were not welcome on their property.

There were no stores on Pirate Island. People called in their orders to Mainland, and the supplies were delivered by boat. During the vacation season the boats ran several times a day. At other times the boats came only a few times a week. Many of the islanders had their own boats.

"There," said Grandpa as he hung up the telephone. "Now we must remember to meet the four o'clock boat."

"We're good at remembering," said Bill.

"What were you planning to build?" asked Grandpa.

"We'll tell you about that later, Grandpa," said Jed. "First you have something to tell us."

"I do?" asked Grandpa. "What?"

"Come on, Grandpa," said Bill. "You know, the story—the Cougar Island story."

"Oh, that," said Grandpa. "I forgot all about it."

"How could you!" said Liza.

"All right," said Grandpa. "Give me a minute to pull my thoughts together."

·5·

The Cougar Island Story

The children were silent. They knew their Grandpa well. He always needed to have a few minutes to pull his thoughts together. But when he started a story, they knew it would be a good one.

"I don't know any of the Cougar family," began Grandpa. "The last one, a son, died when I was a boy, but all of the islanders know their story. The Cougars were very wealthy. During their time the island was like something out of a storybook. They had a large house surrounded by all kinds of beautiful gardens. They also had their own horses and tennis courts. I wish I could have seen it."

"Did your parents ever see it?" asked Bill.

"Just once," said Grandpa. "The Cougars had a big party and invited all of the islanders. My, was everybody excited. The ladies spent hours deciding what they should wear. To them it was the event of a lifetime. That was all they could talk about for months afterward. When the ladies weren't talking about that party, the men were. We children almost felt as if we had been there. That turned out to be the last party Mr. and Mrs. Cougar ever had. Shortly after that they were killed in a boating accident in some foreign country."

"What about the son, Grandpa?" asked Jed. "What happened to him?"

"He's another story," said Grandpa. "Elliot was a strange person. He wanted nothing to do with people. Years would go by without him ever leaving the island. After his parents died he allowed no one other than his lawyer to set foot on the island. They say he used to patrol the island with a gun."

"Sounds like he should have been put away," said Bill. "But how did he get food and stuff?"

"A boat from Mainland went to the island once a month. The crew handed him the things he had ordered. He gave them a list for the next month and that was it. He didn't say one word to them."

"Who paid the bill?" asked Liza.

"That was handled through his lawyer," said Grandpa. "He visited Elliot every week."

"What finally happened to Elliot?" asked Jed.

"His lawyer went over one week and found him very ill," said Grandpa. "He was taken to the hospital in Mainland, and he died there. He was buried on Cougar Island in the family cemetery."

"What happened to all of the Cougar money?" asked Bill.

"Elliot left a will," said Grandpa. "He also left instructions that the will be published in the newspaper at least once a year."

"What!" said Liza. "I never heard of anyone doing that!"

Grandpa laughed and said, "Neither had anyone else. But his instructions have been followed."

"Come on, Grandpa," said Bill. "What did the will say?"

"It said that he was the last of the Cougar family. His money was to be put in trust and used to pay the taxes on the island forever," said Grandpa. "Then he said that the island would always be private property and no one had the right to trespass. If anyone did, it was at their own risk. They would be haunted forever by the ghosts of generations of Cougars who were buried there."

"Wow!" said Bill. "Now, that's some story."

"Grandpa," said Jed. "Did you ever go to the island?"

"I tried it once," said Grandpa, "and I still shiver when I remember what happened."

"Tell us, Grandpa," said Liza.

"My parents told me not to go there," said Grandpa, "but

curiosity got the best of me. I had to find out about that island. One day I took the boat, which I had hidden at my dreaming place, and went over. I had just beached the boat and stepped onshore when the wind became quite strong. Weird moaning noises filled the air all around me. I was terrified! I jumped back into the boat and rowed for my life back to Pirate Island. There I sat on the shore and shook for ages. I wouldn't tell anybody about it because I didn't want my parents to know. It was terrible.''

"And you never went back?'' asked Jed.

"Not on your life,'' said Grandpa. "Once was enough for me.''

"Has anybody ever seen a ghost there?'' asked Liza.

"Some people say they have seen lights moving around at night,'' said Grandpa.

All three children were silent.

"A penny for your thoughts,'' said Grandpa.

"Ghosts or not,'' said Bill, "I want to visit that island.''

·6·

Angry Visitor

Liza glanced out the window.

"Wow!" she said. "Hermit Dan sure looks grouchy."

Grandpa looked and said, "Yes, he is riled about something. I think he's coming here too."

"I'll heat the coffee," said Jed. "That might help."

Soon they heard Hermit Dan coming up the steps.

"Come on in, Dan," called Grandpa.

The door opened. In stepped a bearded man.

"There's a thief on this island!" he shouted.

"What?" said Grandpa. "We've never had any problems before."

"Are you sure?" asked Bill.

"Of course I'm sure," shouted Hermit Dan.

"How about starting at the beginning and telling us what happened," said Grandpa.

"Would you like some coffee, Mr. Dan?" asked Jed.

"Please," said Hermit Dan. "That will help me to get my wits together."

"I'll have some too," said Grandpa.

Jed brought the coffee to the men. Then they all sat quietly waiting for Hermit Dan to tell them what had happened. Finally he pushed his coffee cup away and began to talk.

"First it was eggs," said Hermit Dan. "Then I noticed that I wasn't getting as much milk as usual."

"Isn't this molting season for the hens?" asked Grandpa.

"That's about over," said Hermit Dan, "and that wouldn't bother the cow."

"When did this start?" asked Jed.

"Oh, three or four days ago," said Hermit Dan. "I didn't think anything about it at first. Then today I counted my fryers and one is missing."

"Are you sure?" asked Grandpa.

"Of course I'm sure," said Hermit Dan. "I'm not dotty yet."

"Couldn't an animal have gotten the fryer?" asked Liza.

"It was an animal, all right," said Hermit Dan. "A human animal. I looked all around the pen. There were no signs of digging. An animal couldn't unfasten the gate."

Grandpa shook his head and said, "I sure am sorry to hear all of this."

"Have you seen any of those summer people hanging around this end of the island?" asked Hermit Dan. The children shook their heads.

"They know they aren't supposed to be here," said Bill. "I don't think they would dare. The kids are all scared of you."

"Good," said Hermit Dan. "Let's keep it that way."

"Hey," said Liza. "Maybe it was the rat!"

"Rat? What rat?" asked Hermit Dan.

The children told him about their experience. Hermit Dan shook his head and said, "No, the rat could have taken the eggs and killed the chicken, but there would have been signs left."

"And I don't think a rat could milk a cow," said Bill.

"Speaking of rats," said Grandpa, "it's about time to meet the boat."

"We're on our way," said Liza.

The boys followed Liza out the door. They walked toward the boat landing.

"Well, what do you think?" asked Jed.

"If Hermit Dan says there's a thief, then there is one," said Bill. "I'll bet he counts the vegetables in his garden."

"I know one thing for sure," said Liza. "It wasn't any of the summer people."

"But who was it?" asked Jed.

"That's the mystery," said Bill.

"So let's solve it," said Liza.

"Now, wait a minute," said Bill. "Cougar Island comes first. I meant it when I said that I wanted to visit that island."

"So do I," said Jed. "Don't you, Liza?"

"I'm not sure," said Liza. "Those ghosts sound awfully real to me."

"Then you solve the mystery of the thief," said Bill. "Jed and I will take the island."

"Hold it!" said Liza. "I didn't say no. I just have to think about it."

The boys grinned. They knew Liza wasn't about to be left out of any adventure.

"Hey, the boat is coming in!" shouted Bill. "Let's hurry."

The three broke into a run. They got to the landing just as the boat pulled in.

One of the boatmen called, "Hi, there, I have your package."

"Thank you," said Bill.

"Always at your service," said the boatman. "Are you having a good summer?"

"The best," said Liza.

The boatman started to unload other packages. Liza, Bill, and Jed walked back home.

"So do we start on our raft tomorrow?" asked Bill.

"We can't unless Grandpa gets that rat," said Jed. "You heard what he said."

"I know," said Bill, "but we have most of the stuff outside. Couldn't we at least start?"

"You're right," said Jed. "We could start. Okay, Liza?"

"Huh?" said Liza. "I'm sorry, I didn't hear you. I was thinking."

"About the thief?" asked Bill.

"Yes," said Liza. "I just don't understand it."

"There's probably a simple explanation," said Jed. "Hermit Dan was excited. He could have counted wrong."

"Let's see what Grandpa thinks," said Liza. The three ran to the house.

·7·

Who Did It?

"Hey, Grandpa, I got it," yelled Bill as he rounded the corner to the back porch.

"Gran, you're home," said Liza.

"I just got here," said Gran. "What did you get, Bill?"

"Rat poison," said Bill.

"Oh, Gran," said Liza. "A rat ran across my foot."

The children quickly told Gran their story.

"My goodness," said Gran. "I leave for one day and everything happens."

"It's all right," said Grandpa. "We'll soon take care of that rat."

The children followed Grandpa to the shed.

"You stay outside now," said Grandpa. "I'll handle this."

Jed and Bill began to arrange boards for the raft.

"We need those cross ties," said Jed. "I wish that rat had hidden a few minutes longer."

"I wish it had hidden forever," said Liza.

"What about nails?" asked Bill.

"Grandpa has plenty of those," said Jed. "He won't mind if we use a few."

"Are we going to tell him?" asked Liza.

"Tell him what?" asked Bill.

"About the raft," said Liza.

"I don't know," said Jed. "What do you think?"

"Think about what?" asked Grandpa. "What are you planning? Wait, let me guess. From the looks of the layout you're going to build a raft."

"Good guess," said Bill.

"And you're planning to use that raft to get to Cougar Island," said Grandpa.

"Is that all right?" asked Jed.

"I'll have to think about it," said Grandpa.

"Do you have a better way to get there?" asked Bill.

Grandpa smiled and said, "I might."

"Grandpa," said Liza, "are you saying we can get to Cougar Island without a boat?"

"No," said Grandpa. "I have to do some thinking."

"How long do you have to think?" asked Bill.

"It may take a while," said Grandpa.

"Grandpa!" said Liza.

"Now, don't bug me," said Grandpa. He walked away.

"Is he mad?" asked Bill.

"I don't think so," said Jed. "I think he's teasing us."

"Well, he's not going to put me off," said Bill. "I'm going to Cougar Island some way."

"Take it easy, Bill," said Liza. "Give Grandpa a chance."

"Okay," said Bill. "What do we do in the meantime?"

"Let's go back to the dreaming place," said Jed.

"Not until I change pants," said Bill. "I've had enough scratches for one day."

"That's one reason I wanted to go," said Jed.

"So I could get more scratches?" asked Bill.

"Come off it, Bill," said Jed. "I wanted to cut a path through the bushes."

"Good idea," said Liza. "Let's go."

The children quickly changed into other clothes, got the equipment they needed, and headed for the dreaming place.

"I'll see Cougar Island differently now," said Liza.

"I wonder if there are still moving lights?" asked Bill.

"Could be," said Jed. "I intend to check that out."

"How?" asked Bill.

"I might as well tell you," said Jed. "I plan to go to the dreaming place one night and watch."

"And you were going to leave us behind!" said Liza.

"I thought you didn't want anything to do with ghosts," said Bill.

"I changed my mind," said Liza. "Besides, looking for lights while we are on Pirate Island and they are on Cougar Island is a different thing."

"Are we going to tell Gran and Grandpa?" asked Bill.

"Why not?" said Jed. "Grandpa knows we'll do that. If he minded, he would have warned us."

"He is acting strange about this," said Liza. "It's almost as if he wants us to go to Cougar Island."

"Maybe he wants to go with us," said Jed. "Maybe he knows there's nothing there."

"That makes me feel even better about going," said Liza.

"Here is the dreaming place," said Jed.

"Are you sure?" asked Bill.

"Can't you see where we broke bushes getting in this morning?" asked Jed.

"Yep," said Bill, "but I would have missed it."

"Did we break all of those?" asked Liza.

"Nobody else was here," said Jed.

Liza looked carefully around the bushes. Suddenly she stopped. She pulled a limb back.

"Hey, guys!" she called. "Come here!"

"What is it?" asked Jed.

Liza pointed to a tunnel in the bushes.

"Was that here this morning?" asked Bill.

"I didn't see it," said Liza.

"How did you happen to find it?" asked Jed.

"The bushes looked thinner here," said Liza. "I pulled back this limb and there it was."

"How about that?" said Bill. "Somebody else *does* know about Grandpa's dreaming place."

"Do you think Grandpa did it?" asked Liza.

"No," said Jed. "Grandpa seemed really surprised when we told him we had found it."

Jed stooped down and began looking at something.

"What did you find?" asked Liza.

"This wood wasn't broken," said Jed. "It was cut."

"How can you tell?" asked Bill.

"Take a look," said Jed. "See how smooth it is. It would never break that way."

"I see what you mean," said Bill.

"Is it freshly cut?" asked Liza.

"Not today," said Jed. "It would be wet at the top from the sap. It's been cut for a couple of days."

The children looked at each other. Each had the same question. "Who did it?"

·8·

Sneaky Grandpa

"Let's see if we can find a clue inside," said Liza. One by one the children crawled through the tunnel.

"It looks the same as when we left it this morning," said Bill.

"The moss doesn't hold footprints," said Jed, "so we can't check for those."

"Now what do we do?" asked Liza.

"Thank whoever saved us the work," said Bill, "and go home for supper."

"I guess Bill's right," said Jed. The children left the dreaming place and started home.

"Are we going to tell Grandpa about the tunnel?" asked Liza.

"Let's not," said Bill, "and let's not tell about looking for the lights, either."

"Why not?" asked Jed.

"I want to see what he says," said Bill. "You know how Grandpa likes to second-guess us. It's more fun that way."

"You're right," said Jed. "He would probably be disappointed if we started telling him everything."

"What do you say, Liza?" asked Bill.

"What? Sorry, I wasn't listening," said Liza.

"Thinking your own thoughts, huh?" said Bill. "How about sharing them?"

"Haunted," said Liza.

"Huh!" said Jed. "What does that mean?"

"Remember what a fit I had when I found out that we were moving into a haunted house?" asked Liza.

"I sure do," said Bill. "I also remember what fun we had trying to find out who was supposed to be haunting it."

"That turned out to be quite an adventure," said Jed. "But that was almost a year ago. What does it have to do with this?"

"Now we find a whole island that is supposed to be haunted," said Liza.

"So we'll have another haunted adventure," said Bill. "I hope it's as much fun as our haunted house was."

"We're not going to be haunted," said Jed. "We're going to be hunted if we don't get home for supper."

"Right," said Bill. "Let's go."

They ran toward the house.

"There you are," said Gran. "I was about to send Grandpa out to hunt for you."

The children laughed.

"We got to talking and forgot the time," said Jed.

"Then my stomach reminded me," said Bill, "and we ran right home."

"Get washed up and come to the table," said Gran.

The children went to wash up.

"They are up to something," said Grandpa.

Gran smiled and said, "Aren't they always?"

Everyone was soon seated and serving themselves supper.

"Hey, Gran, is that what I think it is?" asked Bill.

"Is what what you think it is?" asked Gran.

"That beautiful red stuff in the blue bowl," said Bill. "Could it really be raspberry jam?"

"It sure is," said Gran. "I was surprised you didn't ask about it when I came home."

"We had a certain rat on our minds then," said Liza.

"True," said Gran. "Jenny sent the jam for you three."

"Huh?" said Grandpa. "What about me?"

"We'll share," said Jed.

Everyone stopped talking and enjoyed Gran's good supper.

Afterward Liza, Bill, and Jed washed the dishes and cleaned up. Then they joined their grandparents on the porch.

"Thank you very much," said Gran. "I didn't realize how tired that jam making made me."

"Was it worth it?" asked Bill.

"It was," said Gran, "just to see you gobble it down."

"That's my Gran," said Bill.

"Look at that full moon," said Liza.

"Yep," said Grandpa. "It's very relaxing to look at something so beautiful at the end of the day."

"It's too nice a night to waste," said Jed. "Anybody for a walk?"

"I'll go with you," said Liza.

"Count me in," said Bill. "Okay, Gran?"

"I don't know," said Gran. "I'm still concerned about Dan's thief."

"Oh, nonsense," said Grandpa. "Let them go."

"Do take your flashlights, then," said Gran.

"We will," said Jed.

"And you'd better take your sweaters," said Grandpa.

"Sweaters!" said Liza. "As warm as it is?"

"It will get chilly later tonight," said Grandpa. "The ghost lights don't appear until midnight."

"Midnight!" shouted Bill.

"Aha!" said Grandpa. "That is what you're up to."

"Grandpa!" said Liza, "how did you know?"

"Just a lucky guess," said Grandpa. "I knew you were up to something."

"Are you serious," said Bill, "about the lights not coming until midnight?"

"Nope," said Grandpa. "Just wanted to see what you would say."

"Don't be away too long," said Gran.

"We won't," said Jed.

The children got their things and started for the dreaming place.

"That Grandpa!" said Liza. "He gets the best of us every time."

"It is hard to fool him," said Jed.

"He really tricked me into that, though," said Bill.

"It doesn't matter," said Jed. "Let's hurry."

·9·

Ghost Lights

The children were quiet until they reached the dreaming place. Quickly they slipped through the tunnel.

"It's even prettier at night," said Liza. She sat down on the soft moss. Bill and Jed did the same.

"We'll have to be careful," said Bill. "This is so comfortable, I could easily fall asleep."

"We should have brought our sleeping bags and camped out," said Liza.

"Next time," said Jed. "I have a feeling we're going to be doing this again."

"Shhh," said Bill.

"Shhh for what?" asked Liza.

"Listen," said Bill.

Liza and Jed listened.

"Did you hear it?" asked Bill.

"Hear what?" asked Jed.

"It sounded like somebody paddling a boat," said Bill.

They listened again.

"That's just water hitting the bank," said Jed. "The wind is picking up."

"Sounded like a boat to me," said Bill.

"It's easy to imagine things in the dark," said Liza.

Suddenly the silence of the night was broken by a "Yap, yap, yap!"

"Jelly Bean!" cried Liza.

"What's he doing here?" asked Bill.

"Who knows?" said Liza. "Jelly Bean, come here."

Jelly Bean ran to her, yapping all of the way. He pounced on her lap.

"Your feet are wet!" said Liza. "What have you been up to?"

"Did he go home with us this morning?" asked Jed.

"I don't remember," said Bill.

"He didn't come in for supper," said Liza.

"I didn't see him all afternoon," said Jed.

"Hey, Jelly Bean," said Bill, "are you leading a secret life?"

Jelly Bean gave a sleepy yap.

"So much for answers from him," said Bill.

"Back to the lookout," said Jed.

The children sat watching the banks of Cougar Island. A few minutes later Jed said, "Hey, do you see what I see?"

"A ghost light!" said Liza. The three children stared at a small light that moved from place to place.

"It looks like someone beaching a boat to me," said Bill.

"Oh, Bill!" said Liza. "You've got boats on your mind."

"No, wait a minute," said Jed. "I think Bill is right! It does look like that."

"Remember?" said Bill. "It was right after I heard the paddling that Jelly Bean showed up with wet feet."

"So what does one have to do with the other?" asked Liza.

"Use your head, Liza," said Bill. "I think Jelly Bean had a trip to Cougar Island and back by boat."

"Look!" said Jed. "The light is moving. Keep your eyes on it."

The light moved away from the bank and disappeared.

"Think that's it?" asked Bill.

"Keep watching," said Jed.

A few minutes later Liza said, "Look! Up in the air! That's a different light. Maybe it's the real ghost light."

"More likely a firefly," said Bill.

"No," said Jed. "A firefly darts around. That light just flickers."

"I think it is a ghost light," said Liza.

The children watched in silence as the light moved into and out of sight. Then it disappeared. The children waited, but the light was gone.

"I guess the show is over for tonight," said Jed. "Let's go."

"Make sure you have Jelly Bean," said Bill.

"He's sound asleep," said Liza. "I'll probably have to carry him all the way."

"I wish he could talk," said Bill. "Then we would know what all of this is about."

"I'll admit that I'm completely baffled," said Jed.

The children walked along in silence, each trying to sort out the events of the night. Suddenly Jed said, "A candle!"

"A candle!" said Bill. "What's that supposed to mean?"

"That last light was a candle," said Jed.

"Floating in midair!" said Liza.

"I don't understand it, either," said Jed, "but I'm sure it was a candle."

"You just don't want to admit that there are such things as ghost lights," said Bill.

"I said I didn't understand it," said Jed, "but I'm going to find out."

"What do we tell Grandpa?" asked Liza. "You know he's going to ask."

"Tell him the truth," said Jed. "Did you see any ghost lights?"

"I'm not sure," said Liza.

"Then let me answer," said Jed. "I know I didn't see any."

A little later three tired children went into the house. Grandpa was having a cup of coffee.

"Gran gave up on you and went to bed," said Grandpa. "She made some hot chocolate for you, though."

"Just what I want," said Bill. "I'll even serve it."

"Wow, that's a change," said Liza.

"Well, I'm waiting," said Grandpa. "Tell me about the ghost lights. How many did you see?"

"I didn't see any," said Jed, "but there were plenty of stars out."

Grandpa laughed and said, "Better luck next time. I'll see you in the morning."

Grandpa left the children drinking their hot chocolate.

"That was easy," said Bill. "I'm surprised he didn't ask us more."

"I think he was too sleepy," said Liza, "and so am I."

The children rinsed their cups and went to bed.

·10·

Strange Happenings

The next morning the children burst into the kitchen.

"Morning, Gran," said Bill. "Did you sleep well?"

"Like a log," said Gran. "I didn't even hear Grandpa come to bed."

"Where is Grandpa?" asked Liza.

"Here I am," called Grandpa. "I just buried one very dead rat."

"Do you think there are any more?" asked Gran.

"I doubt it," said Grandpa. "I'll leave the poison out for a day or two, just in case."

Gran put the breakfast on the table.

"Oh, boy, ham and eggs!" said Bill. "My stomach is ready for that."

"Bill," said Gran with a laugh, "is there anything you don't like?"

Bill thought a minute and said, "Not if it's food."

After they had eaten Grandpa said, "I agree with Bill. That was a fine breakfast."

The back door opened, and Hermit Dan came in.

"Good morning, Dan," said Gran. "Would you like some breakfast?"

"No, thank you," said Hermit Dan, "but I will have a cup of coffee."

Liza got the coffee for him.

"I came to tell you what fine grandchildren you have," said Hermit Dan.

The children looked at each other. Was this really Hermit Dan giving them a compliment?

"We kind of like them," said Grandpa.

"I want to thank them," said Hermit Dan.

The children looked puzzled. Then Bill said, "Thank us for what?"

Now Hermit Dan looked puzzled as he said, "For weeding my garden. I couldn't have done a better job myself."

"How about that," said Grandpa. "When did you find time to do such a nice thing? I'm proud of you."

Hermit Dan saw the puzzled looks on the children's faces. He asked, "It was you who weeded my garden, wasn't it?"

"I wish we could say yes," said Liza, "but we haven't been near your garden."

"I thought it was off-limits to us," said Bill.

"If you didn't do it, then who did?" asked Hermit Dan. Nobody had an answer to that.

"When was it done?" asked Gran.

"Sometime between yesterday and this morning," said Hermit Dan. "My knees have been stiff for a few days. I haven't been able to weed. You know how fast weeds grow here. I went down this morning to take care of them. The garden was as clean as a whistle."

"Is there anything missing this morning?" asked Gran.

"I haven't checked," said Hermit Dan. He shook his head and said, "I just don't understand what is going on."

"Could we check to see if there are any footprints?" asked Jed.

"No use," said Hermit Dan. "I raked the whole garden."

"That blows that," said Bill.

Hermit Dan finished drinking his coffee and got up.

"I'll go and check the eggs," he said. "Of course, I really can't be sure if any are missing."

"Don't worry, Dan," said Gran. "I'm sure this will clear itself up."

"Just keep your eyes open for any strangers," said Hermit Dan as he left.

A whistle sounded. Grandpa looked at his watch and said, "It's about time. I've been waiting for my paper."

"I'll get it for you," said Liza.

"Thank you, Liza," said Grandpa.

"I'll go with you," said Jed.

"And I'll stay here," said Bill.

Liza and Jed ran out the back door.

"What do you think of Hermit Dan's helper?" asked Jed.

"I don't know what to think," said Liza. "It all sounds very strange."

"I still want to look around that garden," said Jed. "Maybe there is some clue."

"Maybe," said Liza. "Let's take a look after we give Grandpa his paper."

"Out bright and early this morning," said one of the boatmen.

"Grandpa is anxious for his paper," said Liza.

"And well he should be," said the boatman. "Lots of excitement in Mainland."

"What happened?" asked Jed.

"It's on the front page," said the boatman. "Read it for yourself."

Jed reached for the paper.

"Wow!" he said. "The Mainland Bank was robbed. That is big news."

"Did they catch the robbers?" asked Liza.

"No," said Jed. "They think it was the same people who robbed the bank on John's Island a couple of days ago."

"Where is John's Island?" asked Liza.

"I don't know," said Jed, "but it must be close by. They think the robbers are hiding on one of the area islands."

"Do you think they're around here?" asked Liza.

"Could be," said Jed.

"Grandpa is going to wonder what happened to us," said Liza. She and Jed ran home.

"Big news, Grandpa!" called Jed.

"Here, let me see," said Grandpa. He read the story aloud.

"Land sakes!" said Gran. "Who would have thought a quiet area like this would have such troubles!"

"Maybe they're the ones who are robbing Hermit Dan," said Bill. "This is one of the area islands."

"And I guess they weeded his garden," said Liza.

"It doesn't seem likely, does it?" said Bill.

"Do you think the two incidents are related?" asked Grandpa.

"I don't know," said Bill. "None of it makes sense to me."

"I doubt if those robbers are around here," said Gran. "I don't think there are any other banks for them to rob."

"I expect you're right," said Grandpa. "They wouldn't come to this island. It's too small and there are too many people."

"Come on, Liza, Bill," said Jed. "Let's take a walk."

·11·

Wet Pants

When they were outside, Bill asked, "Where to? The dreaming place?"

"No," said Jed. "Let's go by Hermit Dan's garden first."

"Think he might have missed something?" asked Bill.

"It won't hurt to look," said Jed.

"I wish we had been the ones to weed that garden," said Liza.

"Yeah," said Bill. "If only we'd known that he was having trouble with his knees."

"Too late now," said Jed. "But I don't understand why

someone would steal from him, then turn around and weed his garden."

"That's what we need to find out," said Liza.

Hermit Dan was coming out of his garden as the children arrived.

"Good morning again," he said. "I decided to come back and pick the peas."

"Gee," said Liza. "Your garden is clean."

"Whoever did it knows something about gardening," said Hermit Dan. "If I knew who it was, I would offer them a job."

"You would!" said Bill.

"Yep," said Hermit Dan. "Good gardeners are hard to find."

"Mind if we look around?" asked Jed.

"Still looking for clues?" asked Hermit Dan.

"Maybe a footprint or two," said Bill.

"Sorry about that," said Hermit Dan. "There were prints, but I was sure they were yours."

Hermit Dan went on his way. Liza, Bill, and Jed searched the garden for some kind of clue.

"It's no use," said Bill. "All of the evidence was raked away."

"On to the dreaming place?" asked Liza.

"I guess so," said Jed.

"Hey, wait a minute," said Bill.

"What's wrong?" asked Liza.

"I was just thinking about what Hermit Dan said," said Bill. "What made him think those footprints were ours?"

"Good question, Bill," said Jed. "Let's remember to ask him."

"Shouldn't we do it now?" asked Liza.

"It can wait," said Jed. "Maybe we'll have better luck finding a clue at the dreaming place."

"Let's go," said Bill. The children cut through the woods and got there in just a few minutes. They slipped through the tunnel and flopped down on the moss.

"Cougar Island looks so peaceful," said Liza. "Could we have imagined those lights?"

"No way!" said Jed. His eyes searched the island. Then he said, "Hey, look over there! I think I see a house."

Bill and Liza looked where he was pointing.

"I can't tell," said Bill. "It may only be shadows."

"No," said Liza. "It looks too solid for that. I think Jed's right."

"Then I was right about the candle too," said Jed.

"How do you figure that?" asked Bill.

"That light was the right height to be in a second-floor room," said Jed.

"You know," said Liza, "that could be it."

Bill patted the moss around him. He asked, "Did it rain last night?"

"I don't think so," said Liza.

"Then the dew must have been heavy," said Bill. "This moss is wet."

Bill stood up.

"The seat of your pants is soaked," said Liza.

"Right through to the skin," said Bill.

"That's funny," said Jed. "I'm not wet."

"Neither am I," said Liza.

Jed began to pat the moss where Bill had been sitting.

"Strange," he said.

"What?" asked Bill.

"The wetness seems to come to a point," said Jed. He got up and began to break some sticks from the surrounding bushes. Liza knew what he was going to do. She got some sticks too. The two began to outline the wetness with sticks. Bill watched a shape begin to show.

Suddenly Bill yelled, "It's that boat again. Someone beached a boat here."

Liza and Jed looked at the shape.

"It does look like a boat," said Liza.

"That settles it," said Jed. "We're going to Cougar Island, and soon."

"Remember?" said Bill. "Grandpa said he would tell us his idea today."

"He sure did," said Jed. "So much was happening, I forgot about that."

"Let's go ask him now," said Liza.

The children started to leave.

"Oh, drat," said Bill. "I hear Jelly Bean. He sounds as if he has something cornered."

"We'd better take him home," said Jed. "He might disappear again."

"I'll get him," said Liza. She ran toward the barking.

"Oh, no, Jelly Bean!" she yelled. "Bill, Jed, come quickly."

They ran to where Liza was and saw Jelly Bean running around in circles, yapping his head off. And there sat a small yellow kitten looking scared to death.

"How did a cat get here?" asked Bill.

"Beats me," said Jed. "But we have to rescue it."

"You get Jelly Bean," said Liza. "I'll get the cat."

The next time Jelly Bean circled, Jed scooped him up. Liza got the kitten and cuddled it close. Jelly Bean tried to squirm away from Jed, but Jed held him tightly. The children hurried home as fast as they could.

·12·

Welcome Kitten

As they neared the house Liza called, "Gran, Grandpa!"

"In the kitchen, Liza," called Gran. "We're making bread."

The children ran into the kitchen. Liza held out the kitten.

"What a cute kitten," said Gran. "Where on earth did you get it?"

"Jelly Bean found it in the woods," said Bill.

"Maybe it belongs to one of the summer people," said Gran. "You know how cats wander."

"I don't think so, Gran," said Jed. "The summer people aren't allowed to have animals. That's one of Captain Ned's rules."

"Jed's right," said Grandpa. "A few years back Ned had trouble with people abandoning animals when the summer was over."

"Then where did that kitten come from?" asked Gran. "None of the islanders have cats."

"It probably came over on one of the boats," said Grandpa. "They're often kept to catch mice."

"Well, we can't keep it," said Gran. "Jelly Bean wouldn't leave it alone."

"We can't just throw it away, Gran," said Bill.

"Of course not!" said Gran. "You can give it to Jenny Hawkins. She said yesterday how much she wanted a cat."

"Let's go," said Bill.

As they were walking to Mrs. Hawkins's Jed said, "Do you really think it came over on a boat?"

"It could have," said Liza. "But it seems like it would have come to one of the houses. What was it doing in the woods?"

"It probably came over on a boat," said Bill, "but not one of the Mainland boats."

"What do you mean?" asked Jed.

"Think!" said Bill. "What boat keeps cropping up at our end of the island?"

"Yeah," said Liza. "That does make more sense."

"At least the kitten will have a good home," said Jed.

Soon the children were knocking at Mrs. Hawkins's door.

"Good morning," said Mrs. Hawkins. "Please come in."

"We brought you something," said Bill. Liza held out the kitten.

"For me!" said Mrs. Hawkins. "Where did you get it?"

The children told her about finding the kitten in the woods.

"How strange," said Mrs. Hawkins. "There hasn't been a cat on the island since Tabby died last spring."

"Grandpa thinks it might have come over on one of the boats," said Bill.

"That could be," said Mrs. Hawkins. "I have seen them on boats. I'm glad this one escaped. I miss my Tabby so much."

"What happened to Tabby?" asked Liza.

"She died of old age," said Mrs. Hawkins.

Liza handed the kitten to Mrs. Hawkins. The kitten began to purr.

"What a cuddly little thing," said Mrs. Hawkins. She looked at the children and said, "Are you sure you don't want to keep it?"

"We can't because of Jelly Bean," said Liza.

"We have three cats at home in Maxton," said Bill. "I don't think Mom would welcome another one."

"Well, this one is mighty welcome here," said Mrs. Hawkins.

"We have to go," said Jed. "We have some things to do."

"Come back anytime you want to play with the kitten," said Mrs. Hawkins.

"Thanks," said Liza. "We will."

The children left.

"What are those things we have to do?" asked Bill.

"I can't get Hermit Dan's garden off of my mind," said Jed.

"But we looked over every inch of the garden," said Bill.

"Maybe I'm crazy," said Jed, "but I still believe there's a clue in that garden."

"It is a big garden," said Liza. "We could have missed something."

"I doubt it," said Bill. "But let's look, anyway."

·13·

Tomato-red Clue

When they reached the garden, Bill said, "I'm glad Hermit Dan isn't here."

"Why?" asked Liza.

"He would think we were crazy for sure," said Bill.

"Oh, I don't know," said Jed. "I think he would understand. This time let's do things a different way."

"Such as?" asked Liza.

"Each of us will take a third of the garden," said Jed.

"We did that this morning," said Bill.

"Wait," said Jed, "I'm not finished. After we finish our

third, each of us will take another third. By the time we've finished, we will have looked over the garden three times. Okay?''

"Sounds like a big waste of time to me," said Bill.

"It makes sense to me," said Liza.

"Are you with us, Bill?" asked Jed.

"I guess so," said Bill.

The children finished their first third and switched places. The second search was no more successful than the first. They were discouraged as they began to go over the garden once again. Liza and Jed had just finished when Bill shouted, "Whoopee! Come look!"

Bill was standing by a tomato bush. Liza and Jed ran over.

"What? What?" they both asked.

"Right there," said Bill, pointing to a red object.

"A doll's shoe!" said Jed. "How did we miss that?"

"Easily," said Bill. "I almost did. I just happened to shake the bush and it dropped out."

"A lucky shake!" said Jed. He picked up the shoe.

"Whew! It's hot," said Liza. "Let's find some shade."

The children left the garden. They walked toward the woods until they found a cool spot.

"Let me see that shoe, Jed," said Bill. Jed handed Bill the shoe. Bill looked it over carefully.

"It looks familiar," said Jed. "Liza, did you have a doll with shoes like that?"

"I don't think so," said Liza, "but it does look familiar."

"What kind of thief is this?" asked Bill. "One who has a doll and weeds gardens?"

"I know! I know!" said Liza. "Bobby Bear!"

"Bobby Bear!" said Bill. "Who is that? I never heard of him."

"You know, little Mandy," said Liza.

"First you say a Bobby Bear is the thief," said Bill. "Now you say a little Mandy. Liza, I think the sun has gotten to you. You aren't making sense."

"Yes, she is," said Jed. "You mean that stuffed bear Mandy always has with her?"

"Yes," said Liza. "The shoes are always coming off. She asked me to put one back on the other day."

"Mandy? The Mandy at the summer end of the island?" asked Bill. "You think she's the thief?"

"Bill! Stop it!" said Liza. "I don't know, but I do know that Mandy's bear has shoes like that."

"Okay, okay," said Bill. "At least we know something. What do we do now?"

Liza jumped up and said, "Go to the summer end. Find out if Bobby Bear has lost a shoe."

"I've had enough walking for a little while," said Bill.

"So stay here," said Jed. "Come on, Liza, this is the first real lead we've had."

Bill jumped up and said, "Let's go!"

"Thought you were tired," said Liza.

"Thought you were hot," said Bill. They both grinned, each knowing that the other wasn't about to be left out.

The walk to the summer end of the island was a long one. The children didn't say much on the way. Each was hoping that finding the red shoe would help them solve the strange puzzle. Finally they could hear the voices of children at play.

"Maybe we can get the shoe squared away," said Bill, "and play a little ball."

"First things first," said Jed.

"Mandy is first," said Liza. "I see her on their steps."

"Let's go," said Bill.

"Hold it!" said Jed.

Bill looked puzzled as he said, "Hold it for what?"

"You can't go dashing up to her," said Jed. "It might scare her. She's just a little girl."

"So what should we do?" asked Bill. "Tiptoe?"

"Don't act so dumb," said Liza. "Just follow us."

The three walked over to Mandy. Liza said, "Hi, Mandy, where's Bobby Bear?"

"I'll get him," said Mandy. "He's taking a nap."

Mandy ran into the house.

"Will she come back?" asked Bill.

"If not, we know where to find her," said Jed.

Just then the door opened, and out came Mandy with Bobby Bear.

"Hey, look," whispered Bill. "He *is* missing a shoe!"

"How about that!" said Jed. "Maybe we're getting some-place."

"Here's Bobby Bear," said Mandy. "Say hello to him, Liza."

"Hello, Bobby Bear," said Liza. "What happened to his other shoe?"

"He lost it again," said Mandy. "I don't know what I'm going to do with him."

Jed held up the red shoe and said, "Is this it?"

Mandy's eyes brightened as she said, "Oh, you found it. Thank you. Liza, please tie it on real tight."

Liza put the shoe on Bobby Bear.

"Did you like Hermit Dan's garden, Mandy?" asked Bill.

Mandy looked puzzled.

"You know," said Bill, "the garden at the other end of the island with tomatoes and stuff in it."

"Show it to me," said Mandy, taking Bill's hand.

"Didn't you and your parents go to a garden?" asked Jed.

"No," said Mandy. "My parents had to go home."

"Then who is keeping you?" asked Liza.

"My grandma," said Mandy.

"Then did you and your grandma go to a garden?" asked Bill.

"No," said Mandy. "We never go for walks. Grandma doesn't walk very good."

Just then a woman limped out onto the porch and called, "Mandy, come in for lunch."

"Bye," said Mandy. "Thank you for finding Bobby Bear's shoe."

Liza, Bill, and Jed looked at each other.

"So much for that," said Bill. "Now what?"

"It looks as if everyone is going in for lunch," said Jed.

"Lunch!" said Bill. "I forgot all about that."

"Miracles never cease," said Liza.

"I think we're going to need one to solve this mystery," said Jed. "I really thought we had something with that shoe."

"We did," said Liza. "We just didn't have the right Bobby Bear."

"What does that mean?" asked Bill.

"Lots of little kids have those bears," said Liza. "We just haven't found the right one."

"You might have something there," said Jed. "We'll just have to keep trying."

"Let's forget it for now," said Bill. "My stomach just remembered that it was time for lunch."

The children started for home.

·14·

Unexpected Trip

Liza was the first one in the kitchen.

"What's that heavenly smell?" she asked.

"Cinnamon rolls!" shouted Bill.

"Right," said Gran. "Get the plates, knives, butter, and milk. Let's eat them while they're hot."

The children wasted no time in doing as Gran asked. Soon everybody was enjoying hot, buttery cinnamon rolls.

"You spoil us," said Jed.

"I know," said Gran. "That's what grandchildren are for."

"We love it!" said Bill.

"Say, Grandpa," said Jed, "did you think of a way for us to get to Cougar Island?"

"I was wondering when you would ask that," said Grandpa. "I think I have. First I need to ask you some questions."

"Fire away," said Bill.

"Has your father taught you a lot about boats?" asked Grandpa.

"No," said Jed.

"I'm surprised to hear that," said Grandpa. "He loves boating so much."

"He said he didn't have enough patience to teach us," said Bill.

"I expect he's right about that," said Gran. "He *is* short on patience. I remember when he was supposed to be teaching his sisters. He got so mad with Ellen that he dumped her in the lake."

"He didn't!" said Liza.

"Oh, yes," said Gran. "He was in the doghouse for days because of that."

"If you don't know anything about boats," said Grandpa, "that kills my idea."

"But we do know about boats," said Jed. "Dad just said he couldn't teach us. He let us take boating classes. We know enough to satisfy him."

"Then you know a lot," said Gran.

"We've passed our intermediate swimming test," said Liza.

"Do we know enough for your idea, Grandpa?" asked Bill.

"It sounds like it," said Grandpa. He said no more but buttered another cinnamon roll. The children sat quietly as long as they could stand it.

Finally Bill said, "For Pete's sake, Grandpa, what is your idea?"

"I'll show you when you get back," said Grandpa.

"Get back!" said Bill. "Where are we going?"

"Oh," said Gran, "I was just about to tell you. Your mother sent some money for me to take you shopping. She knew you would need a few things by now. I thought we would go to Mainland this afternoon."

"A bathing suit!" said Liza. "That's what I need."

"My sneakers are about to come apart," said Jed.

"You all need new sneakers," said Gran. "Let's try to make the two o'clock boat."

"Wow," said Bill. "We'd better get cleaned up."

"I'll do the kitchen," said Grandpa.

"That will help," said Gran. "I'll get myself ready."

Later Gran and the children walked to the dock. The two-o'clock boat pulled in just as they arrived.

"Good timing," said Jed.

They went on board and found seats for the short trip.

"Let's make a list of the things you need," said Gran. "Then we won't forget anything."

The children told Gran the things they really needed and some other things they just wanted. Gran put them all on the list.

"Do you think there will be enough money for all of that?" asked Liza.

"There may be," said Gran. "I saw in the paper that Harvey's is having a sale. Their prices are very good on sales."

"Great," said Bill. "Maybe we can find everything there. I'm anxious to get back home."

"Come on, Bill," said Jed. "Grandpa wants us out of the way for a while. Right, Gran?"

Gran smiled and said, "He did suggest that we take our time."

"Did he say how long before we could come back?" asked Bill.

"No," said Gran. "He just said not to rush."

"Does that mean we can go to the ice cream shop?" asked Liza.

"Of course," said Gran. "It wouldn't be a trip to Mainland without going there."

"I'm going to have a huge banana split," said Jed.

"Now you're talking my language," said Bill.

"Come on," said Gran. "The boat is about to dock."

"Let's be the first ones off," said Liza.

Harvey's Department Store was three blocks from the dock. Gran and the children headed in the direction of the store. As they drew nearer the sidewalks became more crowded.

"This isn't going to be easy," said Liza. "It looks as if everyone is shopping today."

"Don't worry," said Gran. "We'll manage. Let's take care of the sneakers first."

Gran was right. Despite the crowds taking advantage of the sale, they did manage. In a couple of hours they left the store. All of their arms were filled with packages.

"That was a good shopping spree," said Gran.

"I can't believe we were able to get everything on the list," said Liza.

"Now it's time for my favorite place," said Bill.

·15·

Grandpa's Idea

The ride back to Pirate Island was a quiet one. Everybody was full of ice cream. They felt content to enjoy the short trip. As they were pulling into their dock Jed yelled, "Hey, there's Grandpa!"

"How did he know we would be on this boat?" asked Liza, "Did you tell him, Gran?"

"I did not," said Gran. "I didn't know that myself."

"He must be waiting to tell us his idea," said Bill.

The boat docked. Gran and the children gathered their packages and started off.

"Hey, Grandpa!" said Bill. "Nice of you to meet us."

Grandpa laughed and said, "I didn't come to meet you."

"Then why are you here?" asked Liza.

"For reasons of my own," said Grandpa, "You go on home. I'll meet you there in a few minutes."

"Yes, sir!" said the children.

"I'll walk with Grandpa," said Gran.

The children dashed home and put away their packages. They were waiting impatiently when their grandparents arrived. Grandpa was carrying a long flat package and a big lumpy one.

"Are you ready for my idea?" asked Grandpa.

"Ready!" exploded Bill.

"Are you really going to tell us?" asked Jed.

"Yep," said Grandpa.

"Just like that?" asked Liza.

"If you will give me a chance," said Grandpa. "I found a canoe for you."

"A canoe!" shouted Jed.

"Hooray!" yelled Liza and Bill.

"Where did you get it?" asked Jed.

"I remembered that Captain Ned had one," said Grandpa. "I asked him about it. He was happy to let you borrow it. We took it out to be sure there were no leaks."

"Where is it?" asked Bill. "I'm ready to go."

"Just a minute," said Grandpa. "Let's open these packages. You'll need what's in them."

Liza tore into the lumpy one while Bill and Jed tackled the long one.

"Great," shouted Bill. "These are lightweight oars."

"Thanks, Grandpa," said Jed.

"Thank Captain Ned," said Grandpa. "He suggested them."

Liza giggled as she opened the lumpy package.

"I know who suggested these," she said.

"And well you should," said Gran. "You didn't think you were going out in a canoe without life jackets, did you?"

"Of course not, Gran," said Jed.

"Would we do a thing like that?" asked Bill.

"Off with all of you," said Gran. "I know when I'm being teased."

"I second that," said Grandpa. "Off with you."

The children looked puzzled.

"Off to where?" asked Bill.

"I'll give you one guess," said Grandpa.

"The dreaming place!" shouted the children.

"And be back before dark," said Grandpa.

"Yippee!" shouted the children.

"Cougar Island, here we come!" yelled Bill.

Liza lagged behind the others.

"What's wrong, Liza?" asked Jed.

"Ah, she's scared," said Bill. "She thinks ghosts are floating all over Cougar Island."

"I am not!" said Liza. "Anyway, how do you know ghosts aren't there?"

"Yeah," said Jed. "I feel a little prickly myself."

"Neither of you have to go," said Bill, "but nothing is going to stop me."

Bill ran toward the dreaming place.

"Come on, Jed," said Liza. "He might take off without us."

"He can't," said Jed. "I have the oars."

"In that case, let's dawdle," said Liza.

"Oh, cut it out," said Jed. "We don't have much time."

They reached the dreaming place. There, beached in the center, was the canoe.

"What a great canoe!" said Bill.

"What are we waiting for?" asked Jed. "You two get in and I'll shove off."

"Aye, aye, Captain," said Bill. "Come on, mate."

Bill and Liza got into the canoe. Jed gave one big push. The canoe slid into the water. He jumped in.

"Wow!" said Liza. "This canoe really goes."

"Yep," said Bill. "And each stroke brings us closer to the Cougar Island ghosts."

·16·

Quick Escape

In a few minutes the canoe hit the sandy bottom at the edge of Cougar Island. The children beached the boat.

"Make sure it's all ready to go," said Bill, "in case we need to make a quick getaway."

"Bill!" said Liza. "You really are scared, aren't you?"

"Of course not," said Bill. "I was thinking about you."

"That's a laugh," said Liza.

"Come on," said Jed. "Don't start that. We haven't much time."

"Okay," said Bill. "Which way should we go?"

The children looked all around. Then something caught Liza's eye.

"Look at all those grapes!" she shouted.

"Let's get some," said Bill. He headed toward the grapes.

"Ouch!" he yelled. "We should have worn long pants."

"And sleeves too," said Liza.

"Gran would love to make jelly with those grapes," said Jed.

"Let's remember to bring baskets tomorrow," said Liza.

"Look," said Bill. "There are fruit trees over there."

"I see apples and pears," said Liza.

"The orchard must have been around here," said Jed.

"Fruit trees don't live that long," said Bill, "do they?"

"Maybe they reseeded themselves," said Liza.

"Could be," said Jed.

"I'm going to get some apples," said Bill. "Anybody else coming?"

"Why not?" said Jed. "Coming, Liza?"

"I'm not staying here," said Liza.

The children pushed their way through the thick underbrush. They could see trees that were heavy with fruit.

"Walking isn't too hard," said Bill.

"My scratched legs don't agree," said Liza.

"Think about the fruit," said Jed. "I can hardly wait to sink my teeth into one of those apples."

Suddenly the air was filled with rattling, clattering, and weird moans. Liza and Jed stood frozen in place. Then an earsplitting scream jolted them into action.

"Bill! That was Bill!" whispered Liza.

"Help! Help!" yelled Bill. "They got me! The ghosts have me by my foot."

There was a thrashing in the grass. Then Bill sped by yelling, "Run! Run for your life!"

Liza and Jed raced after Bill. Bill reached the canoe, pushed it into the water, and jumped in.

"Hey, Bill! Wait for us!" yelled Liza, splashing into the water.

"Stop, Bill!" shouted Jed. "Let us in."

Bill stopped paddling long enough for Liza and Jed to climb in. Then he began to paddle furiously.

When she was settled, Liza said, "Bill, you were going to leave us."

"I was scared," said Bill.

"So were we," said Jed.

"Those ghosts were breathing down my neck," said Bill.

"Ghosts don't breathe," said Liza.

"How do you know? It was me they were after," said Bill. "I had to get on the water."

"Why?" asked Jed.

"Because ghosts can't cross water," said Bill.

"I did read that someplace," said Liza.

"We're being silly," said Jed. "Ghosts aren't real."

"And I guess those noises weren't real, either," said Bill.

"Oh, they were real enough," said Jed. "Somebody was trying to scare us."

"They sure succeeded," said Liza.

"Come on, Jed," said Bill. "You could tell that no one had been there recently."

"I still say there's some simple reason for the noises," said Jed.

"Yeah, simple," said Bill. "You didn't get pulled down."

"Bill," said Liza, "you tripped."

"Just drop it," said Jed. "Tomorrow, when we go back—"

"Go back!" said Bill. "I'm not going back!"

"What about you, Liza?" asked Jed.

"I'll let you know tomorrow," said Liza.

"Fair enough," said Jed. "Now, what are we going to tell Gran and Grandpa?"

"The truth!" said Bill.

"Think again, Bill," said Jed. "Remember, I want to go back."

"Yeah," said Liza. "If you make it sound too scary, they won't let us out of their sight."

"Did they ever catch those bank robbers?" Bill suddenly asked. "It could have been them."

"Yipes!" said Liza. "I forgot all about them. Maybe we should tell."

"Listen, guys," said Jed. "We've been though this before.

Let's keep this to ourselves until we find out about the robbers."

The canoe hit the sandy bottom of Pirate Island.

"Okay," said Bill. "I'll agree to anything now that we're on safe ground."

·17·

Mystery Added to Mystery

The children started for home.

"Was what happened real," asked Bill, "or did I imagine it?"

"It seems like a bad dream," said Liza.

"It was real," said Jed, "but I'm sure it ties in with the other things that have been happening."

"Maybe there's a reward for catching those bank robbers," said Liza.

"Hey I didn't think of that," said Bill. "We could get rich!"

"Don't get your hopes up," said Jed. "Ask Grandpa about that."

"Okay," said Bill. "Say, isn't it about time for supper?"

"Supper!" said Liza. "Are you really hungry after those banana splits?"

"Sure am," said Bill. "Those seem like ages ago."

The children were quiet the rest of the way. They had much to think about.

As they got close to the house Bill shouted, "I smell bacon."

He broke into a run. Liza and Jed ran after him.

"Well timed," said Gran. "Dan brought some of his fresh eggs for me to scramble. I don't want them to get cold."

"Hi, Mr. Dan," said Liza. "I love your eggs."

"Then sit down," said Hermit Dan. "Your grandmother asked me to stay for supper."

The children washed up quickly and found their seats at the table.

Grandpa laughed and said, "There's one thing for sure about our grandchildren; *food* is a magic word."

"Grandpa," said Bill, "I need to ask you something. Did they ever catch those bank robbers?"

"Oh, sure," said Grandpa. "They caught them the next afternoon. Why?"

"Just wondering," said Bill.

"I'm surprised you didn't hear us talking about it," said Gran.

"Guess we were busy thinking about other things," said Bill.

"Such as Cougar Island," said Hermit Dan. "I hear you went there this afternoon. How was it?"

"All grown up," said Liza. "It looked as if nobody had ever been there."

"I don't guess anybody has been there lately," said Grandpa.

"I'll never forget the first time I was there," said Hermit Dan.

"When was that?" asked Jed.

"When I was about your age," said Hermit Dan. "I begged my father to let me go. Finally he said he would go with me. Was I excited! When we got there, I started running through the trees. Suddenly I tripped, and down I went. Bells started clanging—"

"Bells clanging!" blurted Bill. "You mean bones clattering!"

Hermit Dan threw back his head and laughed. Then he said, "I can't believe it! Are those bells still working? Were you as scared as I was?"

"I sure was," said Bill. "I thought those ghosts had me."

"Yeah," said Jed. "He took off in the canoe."

"And we had to catch it," said Liza. "He was going to leave us!"

"I can believe it," said Hermit Dan. "I was going to do the same thing. But my dad caught me and held me back."

"You mean he didn't run!" said Bill.

"No, he laughed," said Hermit Dan. "He knew about those bells."

"How did he know?" asked Gran.

"Everybody in Mainland knew about Elliot's bells," said Hermit Dan. "That's why he wouldn't let me go to Cougar Island alone."

"Aren't you going to tell us more?" asked Grandpa.

"After his parents died, Elliot ordered hundreds of bells and rolls of steel cable from Mainland. Then he sent for some workmen to come. I think that's the only time anyone other than his lawyer was allowed on the island. Elliot had found that he couldn't manage that job himself. He had the workmen string bells on the cable and hang them among the trees all around the island. Then he connected the cables to the ground across every path. Somehow he fixed it so that a person walking on the path would trip and set the bells to ringing. It was his alarm system, but I can't believe it's still working."

"Believe it," said Bill.

"But what about the moaning?" asked Liza. "That was weird."

"I didn't hear that," said Hermit Dan. "The trees weren't in leaf when I was there."

"Trees in leaf?" asked Grandpa. "What does that have to do with it?"

"My father heard the moaning," said Hermit Dan. "Your parents may have, too, when they went to the Cougar party. My father asked about it. The Cougars had trees planted all around the island. When they are in leaf, they make a moaning sound when stirred by even a small breeze."

"It was breezy when we were there," said Jed.

"That solves a longtime mystery for me," said Grandpa. "That moaning scared the daylights out of me. How come you never told me all that before?"

"It never came up," said Hermit Dan. "How come you never told me about being scared?"

"I guess I was too ashamed," said Grandpa.

"All right," said Gran. "One of you help me clear the table and get the coffee."

"I'll clear, Gran," said Bill.

Soon that was done, and Gran had served the coffee.

"Do you three want anything else?" asked Gran.

"Nope," said Jed. "Everything was great."

"Especially the conversation," said Bill. "What time did you say we were going in the morning, Jed?"

"Going where?" asked Jed with a big grin. Everybody began to laugh.

Jelly Bean began to yap.

"That's his 'somebody's-coming' yap," said Liza.

"Who could it be at this time of night?" said Gran.

"I'll see," said Bill. He ran to the door and switched on the porch light.

"Thank you for the light," called Mrs. Hawkins.

"Mrs. Hawkins!" said Bill. "Is something the matter?"

Mrs. Hawkins came up the steps. Bill held the door open for her.

"Oh, my, what a time I've had," said Mrs. Hawkins. "Have you seen my kitten?"

"Not since we left her with you," said Bill.

"I was afraid you would say that," said Mrs. Hawkins. "I left the kitten sleeping on a pillow on the screen porch. I left food, water, and a litter box for her. I was gone for a couple of hours. When I got back, she was gone."

"Could she have gotten out of the porch?" asked Gran.

"I don't see how," said Mrs. Hawkins. "I've looked everywhere and called her. I don't know what could have happened."

"I would say it's just mystery added to mystery," said Jed.

"What do you mean?" asked Mrs. Hawkins.

"I don't know exactly," said Jed, "but I'll bet that when we find Mr. Dan's thief, we'll find your kitten."

"There's nothing more anybody can do tonight," said Hermit Dan. "Come on, Jenny, I'll walk you home."

·18·

Threat from the Sky

The next morning at breakfast Jed said, "I meant to ask Hermit Dan if any more stuff was missing from his garden."

"I asked him," said Grandpa. "Yes, he's missing a bit every day."

"He's not mad?" asked Bill. "I thought he would be screaming his head off."

"How is he sure when something is missing?" asked Liza.

"You know Dan," said Grandpa. "He counts certain things and checks the next morning to see what's gone."

"Then why isn't he yelling?" asked Jed.

"Because whoever is taking the vegetables is also working the garden. Dan says they more than pay for what they take," said Grandpa.

"He sure has changed," said Liza. "He had a fit when I took a couple of raspberries."

"Oh," said Grandpa. "I forgot to tell you another strange thing. Dan counted his fryers again and none were missing."

"You mean that one was back?"

"Yep," said Grandpa.

"I wonder if it was really missing in the first place?" asked Liza.

"Dan is sure it was," said Grandpa.

"The missing kitten!" said Liza. "I just remembered. Should we check and see if Mrs. Hawkins found her?"

"We should," said Jed, "but I want to get started for Cougar Island."

"Why don't you call her?" asked Gran.

"Good thinking, Gran," said Bill. "I forget about the telephone here."

"I'll call her," said Liza. Soon she had Widow Hawkins on the line. They talked for a bit. Then Liza hung up.

"Nope," she said, "No kitten. Mrs. Hawkins is really upset about it."

"Keep an eye out for it while you're walking," said Gran. "I still think it wandered off."

"Okay," said Jed. "Is everybody ready?"

"Right with you," said Bill.

"I made a picnic lunch for you," said Gran. "Do you want to take it?"

"Thanks, Gran," said Liza. "We won't have to worry about getting back at any special time."

"Baskets!" said Bill. "Gran, may we take a couple of baskets with us?"

"You know where they are," said Gran. "Take what you like."

"Planning to bring back treasure?" asked Grandpa.

"Just being prepared," said Bill. "Who knows what we'll find."

"You forgot something else, Bill," said Jed.

"What?" asked Bill.

"Long pants," said Jed.

"Thanks, Jed," said Bill. "I'll just be a minute."

"It's scratchy going through the brush," explained Liza to Gran and Grandpa.

As soon as Bill came back they left for their Cougar Island exploration.

When they beached the canoe on Cougar Island, Liza said, "Let's get the fruit first."

"Fine," said Bill. "Then I want to find those bells and see what scared me."

"Suits me," said Jed. "We have plenty of time."

"I'll leave the picnic basket over here," said Liza. "It will stay cooler."

The children once again made their way through the brush to the orchard.

"Oh, the pears are gorgeous," said Liza. "As soon as I fill my basket I'm going to eat one."

"You pick the pears, then," said Jed. "I'll get the apples. I don't think we'll have much help from Bill. He's already wandered off."

A few minutes later Bill yelled, "Hey ho, success! I found the bells."

Liza and Jed ran over to see.

"Where?" asked Liza.

"Look where I'm pointing," said Bill.

"I see them," said Jed. "They are thick with rust."

"That's what made them clatter instead of clang," said Bill.

"That takes care of that," said Liza. "Back to picking pears."

"I'll come in a minute," said Bill. "I want to find something."

Liza and Jed left him. Bill got down on his hands and knees and crawled around.

"It has to be here someplace," he said. "I had to trip on something to make the bells go off."

Bill searched, but he could not find what had tripped the bells. Finally he got up to go join Liza and Jed. Bill took two steps and down he went. The horrible clattering filled the air.

"Help!" he shouted. "They got me again!"

Jed and Liza came running. They expected to find Bill laughing, but he was very angry.

"It's not funny!" he said.

"Are you hurt?" asked Liza.

"If I find what set those bells off, I'll tear it to pieces," shouted Bill.

"Stay put," said Jed. "Maybe I can find it."

Jed began to feel every inch of ground around Bill's feet.

"Aha," he said. "Here it is!"

Bill scrambled around so he could see.

"It's a loop of wire," said Jed.

"Let me pull it out," said Bill. "I don't want those bells to scare anyone else."

Bill pulled as hard as he could. The clattering began again. The more Bill pulled, the louder the bells clattered.

"I give up," said Bill. "I'm going to mark the spot with a stick. Next time I'll bring some wire cutters."

"For now," said Liza, "help us finish getting the fruit."

In a short time the baskets were full.

"Let's leave these by the canoe," said Jed.

"Now we are free to explore!" said Bill.

Just as they were nearing the canoe a rumble sounded from above.

"Is that thunder?" asked Liza.

"It sure is," said Jed, "and if you look up, you'll see a very dark cloud coming our way."

"Uh-oh," said Bill, "you know how Gran and Grandpa feel about being out in a thunderstorm."

"Yep," said Jed. "We had better try to make it home."

"But we didn't get any grapes!" said Liza.

"Next time," said Jed. "Everybody in!"

The children paddled as hard as they could. They made it to Pirate Island in record time.

"Grab a basket of fruit, Bill," said Jed.

"Hey, this is heavy," said Bill.

"I'll take a turn," said Liza.

"Hold it," said Jed. He took off his shirt and piled fruit on it. Then he tied it into a bundle.

"Here, Liza," he said. "This will make it lighter for everybody."

"Why don't we just go to the cave?" said Bill. "We can have lunch there."

"Lunch!" said Liza. "I left the picnic basket on Cougar Island."

"That does it," said Bill. "We have to make it home. Even if we could go back to the island now, those sandwiches would be soggy!"

The children put all of their efforts into walking. The thunder sounded louder.

"Think we'll make it?" asked Liza.

"All we can do is try," said Jed.

Just as they got to the backyard the rain began to come down. Gran was standing at the back door.

"Thank goodness you're here," she said. "Grandpa and I were really worried."

The children ran onto the porch.

"Hey, Grandpa," called Bill. "Come see the treasure!"

"Apples! Pears!" said Grandpa. "Now that's my kind of treasure."

"And mine too," said Gran. "Where did you find it?"

"The Cougar Orchard," said Liza. "There are grapes there too."

"We'll get some next time," said Jed. "That thunder sent us running."

Just then the sky lit up with a jagged streak of lightning.

"Inside, quickly!" said Gran.

·19·

Another Red Shoe

The storm lasted for quite some time before it rumbled away in the distance.

"Now for some lunch," said Gran.

"Gran," said Liza, "I left ours on Cougar Island. Will the rain hurt the basket?"

"Not a bit," said Gran. "The birds can enjoy the sandwiches."

Liza helped Gran get lunch on the table.

"Do you think it's going to rain anymore, Grandpa?" asked Jed.

Grandpa looked out of the window. He said, "That sun looks mighty bright now. But at this time of the year it can change in a few minutes."

"I'm willing to take a chance," said Bill. "I've got some unfinished business to tend to."

"The buildings on Cougar Island are made of stone," said Grandpa. "There's plenty of shelter. If you hear thunder, don't take any chances. Find shelter."

"That we'll do," said Jed.

"I'll take care of cleanup," said Gran. "You all get back to your exploring."

"Thanks, Gran," said Jed. "Let's go."

The children ran outside.

"Wait a minute," said Bill. "I'll get the wire cutters."

Bill got them, and they started for the dreaming place.

"Oh, no!" said Liza. "We forgot to turn the canoe over. It will be full of water."

"No big deal," said Bill. "We'll dump it out."

It wasn't long until the children had the canoe ready and were on their way to Cougar Island.

"I want to cut that wire first thing," said Bill. "Then I can leave the wire cutters in the canoe."

"After that," said Liza, "let's try to find the house. "I'm really anxious to see that."

"Okay to both," said Jed. "Grandpa talked as if there were lots of buildings."

As soon as they had beached the canoe Liza said, "I'll get those sandwiches out of the basket."

She ran over to the basket.

"That's strange," she said.

"What?" asked Bill.

"The basket isn't wet," said Liza.

"That couldn't be," said Jed. "I know it rained here. Let me see."

Jed felt the cloth that covered the basket.

"Dry as a bone," he said. He pulled off the cloth. The three children stared.

"Grapes," said Liza. "The basket is filled with grapes."

"The Cougar Island ghosts have struck again," said Bill.

"At least they seem to be friendly ghosts," said Jed.

"This reminds me of a ghost story I read," said Liza. "Every time the ghost took something, it gave something in return."

"I don't feel afraid," said Jed, "but I don't like all of this. How do you feel?"

"I don't feel afraid, either," said Liza. "I'm more curious than anything."

"The only thing on my mind," said Bill, "is that wire. Let's cut it. Then I'll think about this."

The children started toward the orchard. Bill ran over to where he had fallen.

"Okay, you clattering things," he said. "You've clattered for the last time."

Bill looked all around. He said, "I'm sure this is the place. Where is that stick?"

The three looked all around the area. There were lots of sticks, but they were all on the ground. None marked the place where the wire was.

"Maybe the wind blew it down," said Liza.

"Not a chance," said Bill. "I really stuck it in the ground to stay."

"I guess it's the Cougar Island ghosts again," said Jed.

"Something got it," said Bill.

"I think I know what," said Liza. She leaned down and picked up something. She said, "Does this look familiar?"

"Another red shoe!" said Jed.

"Besides the Cougar Island ghosts," said Bill, "we now have the Pirate Island thieves."

·20·

Swoosh

"At least we're making progress," said Jed. "I'd say that the ghosts and the thieves are one and the same."

"We should have known that before," said Bill.

"How?" asked Liza.

"The boat," said Bill. "They could get from one island to the other as quickly as we do."

"But how could we have known that they were on Cougar Island?" asked Liza.

"Come on, Liza, think," said Bill. "Remember how I heard that boat shortly after Hermit Dan started missing things?"

"That's right," said Jed. "But how do we know it's not one person?"

"Those dumb bear shoes!" said Bill. "There must be a little kid in on it?"

"You're right," said Jed. "Come on, let's find that house. Maybe that's where they're staying."

"Be careful," said Bill. "There may be more of those bells around."

"It would be like us to set them off," said Liza. "Then we would never find those thieves."

"We have to take that chance," said Jed.

The children walked in the direction they thought the house should be. Each had a prickly feeling of excitement. Each expected something big to happen.

After walking for several minutes Jed whispered, "I see it."

Liza and Bill caught up with Jed. They, too, could see a large house.

"If anybody is staying there," said Bill, "we should see signs of a path."

"Look for trampled grass or broken bushes," said Jed.

The children looked carefully. But the only signs they saw were ones they had made themselves.

"Shoot!" said Bill. "Let's go to the house and knock on the door."

Liza and Jed laughed. Liza said, "Do you really think anyone would answer?"

"Then we can break the door down or smash a window," said Bill.

"You know we can't do that," said Jed.

"So what is your plan?" asked Bill.

"First we'll see if the door is locked," said Jed. He started walking toward the front door. Liza and Bill followed him. Jed reached the door. He turned the knob and pushed. The door began to open. The children held their breath. Jed pushed the door open wider.

Suddenly—*SWOOSH*! Something white floated down.

"Yeeee-owww!" screamed the children. They almost pushed each other down as they ran away, each expecting to be grabbed.

When nothing happened, they stopped. They turned and looked back.

"That really was a ghost!" said Liza.

"That's what somebody wanted us to think," said Jed.

"They convinced me," said Bill. "Let's go home. They can *have* Cougar Island."

"No way!" said Jed. "I'm going to get to the bottom of this."

"Jed!" said Liza. "You're going back!"

"Right now," said Jed. He started toward the house.

"He can't go alone," said Liza.

"I guess not," said Bill. They slowly followed Jed. Jed reached the door. He began to laugh.

"Hey," he called. "Come see the ghost."

Liza and Bill ran to join him.

"A sheet!" said Bill. "Let me see that thing."

The children went into the house.

"That looks like something we would make," said Jed. "See how they have it tied over that beam? When the door opens, it comes down."

"That does it," said Bill. "Let's search this house. We'll find whoever is trying to scare us."

"Okay," said Liza, "but let's do it together."

The old house echoed every sound the children made.

"This place feels haunted," said Jed.

"It's downright creepy," said Bill.

"Let's get on with the search," said Liza. "I want to get that done. I really do feel scared now."

The children quickly searched the house, upstairs and down. They found nothing.

"What now?" asked Liza.

"Can't ghosts make themselves visible and invisible?" asked Bill.

"I've read stories about ghosts," said Liza, "but I don't really know much about them."

"I think our ghosts will be very visible," said Jed, "when we find them."

"Can't you imagine how grand this house was?" asked Liza, "Isn't that staircase real marble?"

"It looks like it," said Jed. "I would like to take a long look at everything."

"The wind is really picking up," said Bill. "Listen to those trees moan."

"Think we'll have another storm?" asked Liza.

"Could be," said Jed, "but we have shelter."

"Storm or no storm," said Liza, "I'm going to poke around."

·21·

A Scare for Liza

Liza went from room to room, peeking into every nook and cranny. It grew darker, the wind howled, and rain began to fall. As there was no lightning or thunder, Liza didn't notice it. She was lost in her dream of how the house had looked in better times.

The boys were upstairs making discoveries of their own.

"This place is like a museum," said Bill. "Look at the carvings on this mantel."

"Did you notice the ceiling?" asked Jed. "Those carvings seem to tell a story."

"Wow," said Bill. "It must have taken forever to build this house."

Jed noticed something on the floor. He leaned over to take a closer look.

"Bill, come take a look at this," he said.

"You found something?" asked Bill.

"Yeah, take a look," said Jed. He pointed to the floor.

"Spots on the floor!" said Bill. "Haven't you ever seen spots before?"

"Not spots," said Jed. "Blobs of wax."

"Blobs or spots," said Bill, "who cares."

"I do," said Jed. "It's candle wax. It proves that I was right."

"About what?" asked Bill.

"Remember when we were looking for ghost lights?" asked Jed. "The last one we saw flickered, and I said it was a candle. The one that looked like it was floating in midair?"

"It was in this room!" said Bill.

"Right," said Jed. "Remember how it appeared and disappeared? Look at all the windows in this room."

"Let's see where the blobs lead," said Bill.

The boys studied the floor. Every so often they saw a small blob of wax.

"I'll bet there's some in that next room too," said Jed.

Bill opened the door. He said, "Wow! This whole room is carved panels. Come and see."

"In a minute," said Jed. "I want to tell Liza about the wax."

"She will want to see this too," said Bill.

Jed went to the top of the stairs. He called, "Liza, we have something to show you. Come on up."

"Okay," called Liza. "I want to look at something first."

"Hurry up, then," said Jed.

There was one door Liza hadn't opened. When she did, she found a closet.

"What a large closet," she said. She walked in to get a better look. Suddenly the door banged shut. Liza was all alone in the dark. Liza felt all over the door, trying to find the knob. But there was none.

"Help!" yelled Liza. "Help!"

But no help came. Liza yelled some more. Then she began to cry.

Upstairs Bill said, "Where is Liza? What's taking her so long?"

"I don't know," said Jed, "I'll call her again."

Jed went into the hall and yelled, "Liza, hurry up! What are you doing, anyway?"

There was no answer.

Jed yelled for her again. Still no answer.

"We had better look for her," he said.

The boys ran downstairs, calling Liza. They ran from room to room.

"Where could she be?" asked Bill.

"Wait a minute," said Jed. "Listen!"

The boys heard a faint call. "Help!"

"Keep yelling, Liza," called Bill. "We're coming."

"This way!" said Jed. The call became clearer as the boys neared the closet. Bill quickly opened the door. Liza burst out crying.

"I was so scared," she said.

"What happened?" asked Jed.

"I walked into the closet," said Liza, "and someone slammed the door."

"Did you see anyone?" asked Bill.

"No," said Liza. "It happened so fast."

"Then how do you know it was anyone?" asked Jed.

"The door couldn't close itself!" yelled Liza.

"Don't yell at me," said Bill. "I didn't do it."

Jed was studying the door. He said, "There was no way she could get out."

"Didn't you hear me?" asked Liza. "I yelled and yelled."

"Look at how thick this door is," said Jed. "We were upstairs. We could hardly hear you down here."

"Let's go home," said Liza. "I never want to see this place again."

"Hey," said Bill, "did we leave the front door open?"

"I don't remember," said Jed. "Do you, Liza?"

"No, I don't," said Liza.

"I guess we could have," said Bill. "We were kind of excited."

"Then that might be the answer," said Jed.

"What do you mean?" asked Liza.

"That wind was strong," said Jed. "If the door was open, it could have blown the closet door shut."

"Could that have happened, Liza?" asked Bill.

"I don't know," said Liza. "I just want to go home. I hate this place."

·22·

A Streak of Yellow

Liza had calmed down by the time they got back to Pirate Island.

"Nobody will ask why the basket didn't get wet," said Bill. "That last rain soaked it."

"But we did get the grapes," said Jed.

The children had just about reached the cave when Liza said, "Wait a minute!"

"What is it?" asked Bill.

"I think I saw a streak of yellow," said Liza.

"The kitten!" said Jed. "Where was it?"

"Over this way," said Liza. She walked over to the bushes, softly calling, "Kitty. Here, kitty."

A tiny meow answered her call. The yellow kitten walked out of the bushes. Liza picked her up, The kitten began to purr.

"Widow Hawkins will sure be glad to see you," said Liza.

"Let's take her there now," said Jed.

"How about dropping these grapes off first," said Bill. "They're heavy."

"Sorry," said Jed. "Let me take a turn. We can leave them on the porch while we take the kitten."

When they reached the backyard, Jed went ahead and put the grapes on the back porch. Soon he caught up with Liza and Bill.

As they were walking Jed said, "You know, we've found that kitten close to the cave both times."

"I hadn't thought about that," said Bill. "Do you think the cave has anything to do with the mysteries?"

"I wouldn't be surprised," said Jed.

"Could the cave be the hideout for the Pirate Island thieves?" asked Liza.

"It could be," said Jed. "I intend to find out."

"How?" asked Bill.

"I think we should hide close by tonight," said Jed.

"But will Gran and Grandpa let us?" asked Liza.

"I don't see why not," said Bill. "They've let us sleep out before."

"All of these strange things weren't happening then," said Jed.

"It won't hurt to ask," said Bill.

"We'll find a way," said Jed.

"There's Widow Hawkins," said Liza.

"Mrs. Hawkins!" yelled Bill. "Wait!"

The children ran to Mrs. Hawkins.

"We found the kitten," said Liza.

"Thank goodness," said Mrs. Hawkins. "I've been so worried about her."

"We know," said Liza. "That's why we brought her straight to you."

"This time I'll keep her in the house," said Mrs. Hawkins. "I'll give her time to know it's her home."

"We've got to go," said Jed. "Gran and Grandpa don't know where we are."

"Thanks again," said Mrs. Hawkins.

The children walked back home.

"Hi, Gran," called Bill. "We're here."

"I saw your basket on the porch," said Gran. "I was wondering where you were."

"We found the kitten," said Liza. "We took her to Widow Hawkins."

"I had a feeling that kitten would show up," said Gran.

Grandpa came into the kitchen. He asked, "How was your day?"

"It was exciting," said Jed. "You and Gran really should see that house. It's like a museum."

"Yeah, Grandpa," said Bill. "There are lots of carvings and stuff."

"I would like to see it," said Grandpa. "Gran wants some more of that fruit. Maybe we can plan a picnic."

"Fruit!" said Liza. She ran out on the porch and got the picnic basket.

"Grapes!" said Gran. "I'll call Mainland first thing in the morning and order sugar. These will make grand jelly."

"Say, Gran," said Bill, "can we sleep out tonight?"

"Goodness, no," said Gran.

"Why not?" asked Bill.

"I'm not going to let you spend the night that far away," said Gran. "You might get sick or something."

"Far away?" asked Liza.

"Yes," said Gran. "Cougar Island is too far away to suit me."

"Cougar Island!" said the children. They began to laugh.

"We didn't mean there," said Jed. "We just wanted to go to the cave."

"Oh," said Gran. "That's different. All I've heard lately is Cougar Island."

"Then can we go?" asked Bill.

"If your Grandpa says it's all right," said Gran.

"I don't see why not," said Grandpa. "They've done it before."

"Yippee!" said the children.

"Do you want to have supper before you go?" asked Gran.

"Sure," said Jed. "We're in no hurry."

"We don't want to go until after dark," said Bill.

"Why after dark?" asked Grandpa.

"It's a new game," said Liza, "and it's more fun after dark."

"I should have guessed that," said Grandpa. "You never seem to run out of games."

"Do you need any help, Gran?" asked Bill.

"No," said Gran. "Everything is under control."

"Then we'll get our things together," said Jed.

·23·

Children in Trouble

Later that evening Bill said, "It's getting dark now. Shouldn't we go?"

"Anytime," said Jed.

"Do you have sweaters?" asked Gran.

"Yep," said Liza. "Sweaters, sleeping bags, and lanterns."

"Then have a good time," said Grandpa.

"Thanks," said Jed. "We'll see you in the morning."

When they were on their way, Bill asked, "Why did we really want to wait until after dark to go?"

"We don't want whoever it is to see us," said Jed. "The darkness will keep us hidden."

"Then you really do think someone is using the cave," said Bill.

"We'll never know if we don't try to find out," said Jed.

"Won't they see our lanterns?" asked Liza.

"The moon is so bright, we won't need them," said Jed.

"Won't they hear us walking?" asked Bill.

"Not if we don't make any noise," said Jed. "We'll creep along."

"This is turning into a game," said Liza. "One I hope we win."

As the children neared the woods Jed said, "Okay, stay close together. Try not to make any noise."

The children made their way toward the cave. Suddenly the silence was broken.

"Blast it!" yelled Bill as he crashed to the ground.

"Shhh!" said Liza.

"Shhh, yourself," said Bill.

"Are you okay?" asked Jed.

"Yes," said Bill, "but why is it always me who trips?"

"Just bad luck," said Liza.

"Sorry I spoiled things," said Bill.

"You didn't spoil anything," said Jed. "We'll lay low for a few minutes. Then we'll move on."

Later Liza said, "Can't we go now? I'm getting sleepy sitting so quietly."

"Then let's move," said Jed. "Stick close together."

"Are we going to the cave?" asked Bill.

"No," said Jed. "That clump of bushes near the top of the cave."

"Why not the cave?" asked Liza.

"I have a feeling about that cave," said Jed. "It may be their headquarters."

"To the bushes, then," said Bill. "We don't want to get caught inside."

"Shhh," said Liza. "We're getting close."

The children inched their way toward the cave. The moonlight was bright. The going was easy. Soon they were in the bushes with a clear view of the path leading to the cave.

They had just gotten settled when Liza whispered, "Look! Over toward the garden!"

The moonlight outlined glowing figures moving toward the cave.

"I don't believe it!" said Bill. "Those really *are* ghosts."

"It's only the moonlight and their flashlights," said Jed. "A full moon does crazy things to light."

"I couldn't run, anyway," said Liza. "I'm too scared."

The figures moved closer. The children could hear voices. They could hear someone crying. Finally they were able to make out words.

"Carrie, we can't go on this way," said a boy. "Daniel's cold is getting worse. We have to give up."

"But they'll separate us," said Carrie. "We have to think of something. Please, Mark, try."

Liza, Bill, and Jed were almost holding their breath as they listened. They could hear a young child coughing and wheezing.

"That kid is really sick," whispered Bill.

"They're in trouble," whispered Jed.

"What should we do?" whispered Liza.

"Why don't we just ask them what's wrong?" said Bill.

"That might scare them," said Jed.

By this time the children were in the cave. Liza, Bill, and Jed could hear Daniel wheezing.

"I know," whispered Liza. "Let's take our sleeping bags and go to the cave. After all, we did plan to sleep there."

"Good idea!" whispered Bill. "We can pretend to be surprised to find them there."

"Let's go," whispered Jed.

The children went as quietly as they could. They put on their lanterns and headed for the front of the cave.

"It's a great night to sleep out," said Liza.

Bill walked over to the entrance of the cave and looked in. He called, "Somebody beat us here."

"Maybe they will let us join them," said Jed.

Liza ran to the cave. She said, "Hi, I'm Liza Roberts. These are my brothers, Bill and Jed."

"I'm Mark Adams," said Mark. "This is my sister, Carrie, and my brother, Daniel."

"Can we come in?" asked Bill.

"Sure," said Mark.

Liza, Bill, and Jed crowded into the cave.

"We're spending the summer with our grandparents," said Liza. "Are you here for the summer?"

"No," said Mark. "We don't belong on this island."

"Mark!" said Carrie.

"It's no use, Carrie," said Mark. "You know they were snooping around on Cougar Island."

"I know," said Carrie. "We enjoyed the sandwiches you left."

"They were the best thing we've had to eat lately," said Mark.

"I want some more," said Daniel.

"Soon, Daniel," said Mark.

"Did you see us on Cougar Island?" asked Bill.

"Yes," said Mark. "We were going to get some fruit when one of you set those bells off."

"Did you pull up the stick I left by that wire?" asked Bill.

"I sure did," said Mark. "We needed those bells to warn us."

"Did you take Jelly Bean to Cougar Island?" asked Liza.

"Is that the little black dog?" asked Carrie.

"Yes," said Liza.

"We didn't mean to take him," said Mark. "Daniel slipped him in the boat. I brought him back, though. Is he all right?"

"He's fine," said Bill. He told Mark about hearing the boat and Jelly Bean appearing shortly afterward.

"Did you shut me up in the closet?" asked Liza.

"Why would I do that?" asked Mark.

"I guess the wind did blow the door shut," said Liza.

"We knew you would go to the house," said Mark, "but we weren't there."

"We were in our hideout," said Carrie.

"Your hideout!" said Bill. "Where is that?"

"It's hidden away from the other buildings," said Carrie. "We found it by accident. It's a small cottage."

"Why didn't you stay in the big house?" asked Jed.

"We did for a few nights," said Mark.

"It was too scary," said Carrie. "There were all kinds of creaks and rattles."

"We know you're in trouble," said Bill. "We want to help you."

"You can't," said Mark. Carrie began to cry.

"It must be big trouble," said Jed.

"It is," said Mark. "Much too big for children to handle."

"Could you tell us what it is?" asked Liza.

"It wouldn't do any good," said Mark.

"We may not be able to help you," said Bill, "but Gran and Grandpa can solve any problem."

"Come on home with us," said Liza. "They will help you. They will know how to help Daniel's cold too."

Just then Daniel had a bad coughing spell. He almost lost his breath.

"I don't feel good," he said.

"That does it, Carrie," said Mark. "We have to get medicine for Daniel."

"I know," said Carrie.

"Don't worry, Carrie," said Bill. "It will be all right."

The children started to go. Suddenly Daniel said, "Bobby Bear! I need Bobby Bear!"

"I'll get him," said Mark. He went back in the cave and got Bobby Bear.

"What happened to his shoes?" asked Bill.

"Bobby Bear lost them," said Daniel.

"Did he lose both of them at the same time?" asked Jed.

"No," said Carrie. "He lost one a few days ago. I think he lost the other one today. They kept coming off."

"It's all right," said Daniel. "He doesn't need shoes in the summer. But I need my kitten!"

"She's lost too," said Mark.

"I know where she is," said Liza. "You'll see her in the morning."

Daniel took Liza's hand. He said, "I like you."

·24·

The Whole Story

As they neared the house Mark asked, "Will they really help us?"

"Did you kill somebody?" asked Bill.

"Of course not!" said Mark.

"Then don't worry," said Bill.

"I'm glad you found us," said Carrie.

"Me too," said Daniel.

"Gran, Grandpa," called Jed. "We're home and we brought company."

"It looks like there's already company there," said Bill. "I see Hermit Dan and Mrs. Hawkins."

When they reached the door, Grandpa said, "Come in, come in. Who do we have here?"

"This is Mark, Carrie, and Daniel," said Liza.

Just then Daniel began to cough.

"Oh, my," said Mrs. Hawkins, "that sounds bad."

"Come here, Daniel," said Hermit Dan. "You know, my name is Daniel too."

"It is?" said Daniel, walking toward Hermit Dan.

"But they call me Dan," said Hermit Dan. He picked up Daniel and sat him on his lap.

"I haven't seen you around before," said Hermit Dan.

"Of course not!" said Bill. "These are the Cougar Island ghosts."

"What!" said Grandpa.

"And also Mr. Dan's thieves," said Bill.

"What!" said Hermit Dan.

"We didn't mean any harm," said Carrie. She began to sob. Gran quickly took Carrie in her arms.

"Of course you didn't," said Gran. "Now, how about telling us the whole story?"

Gran sat down and pulled Carrie onto her lap.

"We ran away from our foster home," began Mark.

"Oh, my!" said Mrs. Hawkins. "Were the people mean to you?"

"No!" said Carrie. "They were super."

"Go on, Mark," said Grandpa.

"Our parents were killed two years ago in an automobile accident. There was no one to take us. We were put in a foster home. Mr. and Mrs. Kenny were great to us. Then they had to move to another state to care for Mrs. Kenny's parents. They couldn't take us."

"You didn't want another foster home?" asked Grandpa.

"It wasn't that," said Mark. "Our social worker couldn't find one that would take all three of us. We can't be separated!"

"Of course not!" said Mrs. Hawkins.

"Is your social worker looking for you?" asked Grandpa.

"Not yet," said Mark. "The Kennys left their furniture in the house. The movers will pick it up next week. The social worker was to pick us up a few days before the Kennys left. But she called and said she would pick us up the day they were to leave. The Kennys weren't home when she called. Then they decided to leave early. We didn't tell them about the call."

"That's when we made our plans," said Carrie. "We were packed and ready to go. The Kennys went out to do some last-minute errands. While they were gone we wrote a note saying we had been picked up early."

"Then we hid until the Kennys left later that day," said Mark. "We left a window open so we could get back in the house. Carrie wrote a note to the social worker saying that the

Kennys had taken us with them after all. Carrie told her the Kennys would get in touch later.''

"But why did you go to Cougar Island?'' asked Bill.

"Shortly after we moved to Mainland we heard the Cougar story,'' said Mark. "A neighbor was related to the Cougar lawyer. He took Dad all over the island. Not too long before Dad was killed, he took me to the island. It seemed like a good place to hide.''

"Where did you get the boat?'' asked Jed.

"It was Dad's,'' said Mark. "That was the only thing I asked to keep. The Mainland harbor people let me keep it there. They knew Dad had taught me all about boats.''

"Mark told them we were moving,'' said Carrie. "Then he took the boat down the shore to where we were waiting. He picked us up and we went to Cougar Island.''

"But I never heard a motor,'' said Liza.

Mark laughed and said, "That's because we ran out of gas. I took the motor off and we had to row.''

A sleepy voice came from Hermit Dan's lap as Daniel said, "Can you make things all right?''

"We'll sure try,'' said Hermit Dan.

"Who is your social worker?'' asked Mrs. Hawkins.

"Ms. Marsh,'' said Carrie.

"Jean Marsh?'' asked Mrs. Hawkins.

"Yes!'' said Mark. "Do you know her?''

"I've known her all of her life,'' said Mrs. Hawkins. "Her mother and I were in school together.''

"This little guy is sound asleep," said Hermit Dan.

"Can you carry him?" asked Mrs. Hawkins.

"Carry him where?" asked Bill.

"Why, to my house," said Mrs. Hawkins.

"Why can't they stay here?" asked Bill.

"Because I need to doctor Daniel's cold," said Mrs. Hawkins. "These two need a hot bath and some hot food."

"Gran can take care of that," said Liza.

"Your grandmother has the three of you," said Mrs. Hawkins. "I love children too."

"I never thought a hot bath would sound so good," said Mark.

"And hot food!" said Carrie.

"I'm sorry we stole food from you, Mr. Dan," said Mark.

"You more than paid for it with all the work you did," said Hermit Dan. "Did you take a chicken?"

"We brought it back," said Mark. "We couldn't kill it."

"I just wanted to make sure I counted right," said Hermit Dan.

"Let's go," said Mrs. Hawkins. "We'll see you folks tomorrow."

Hermit Dan, Mrs. Hawkins, and the children started out of the door calling, "Good night and thank you."

"They were really scared when we found them," said Jed.

"You did the right thing to bring them here," said Grandpa.

"Will anything happen to them for running away like that?" asked Liza.

"I don't think so," said Gran. "Who could punish children for wanting to stay together?"

"Oh," said Liza. "Daniel forgot Bobby Bear."

"Bobby Bear!" said Grandpa. "Who is Bobby Bear?"

Bill laughed and said, "I asked the same question a couple of days ago. It's a long story."

"I would like to hear it," said Grandpa.

The children took turns telling Gran and Grandpa the events of the few days.

"You children amaze me," said Grandpa. "I had no idea what you were up to. I was sure you were playing some game."

Gran laughed as she said, "And I thought we knew our grandchildren so well."

·25·

Happy Tears

The next morning the children ran downstairs. Gran and Grandpa were finishing their coffee.

"We must have overslept," said Liza.

"You needed the rest," said Grandpa. "Yesterday was an exciting one for you."

"It sure was," said Jed. "We solved the mystery of the Pirate Island thieves and the Cougar Island ghosts."

"And it turned out to be one big mystery," said Bill.

After breakfast Liza said, "Gran, may we go to Mrs. Hawkins and see the kids?"

"I think you had better wait," said Gran. "I expect that they slept late too. I know Jenny will be calling their social worker. They may need some time alone."

"You're right," said Liza. "I'm anxious about them."

"They will let us know something as soon as they can," said Grandpa. "They sure are plucky children."

"I wonder if we would have done the same thing?" asked Bill.

"You would have done something," said Grandpa. "You wouldn't have given up without a fight."

Liza, Bill, and Jed were restless. They couldn't get interested in anything. Finally they sat on the back steps and waited, hoping some news would come soon.

It wasn't too long before they saw the children, Mrs. Hawkins, and Hermit Dan coming.

"Let's go meet them," said Bill. "I can't wait."

The three jumped up and ran. Bill yelled, "Do you know anything yet?"

"No," yelled Mark. "We're still waiting."

Daniel ran up to Liza and said, "I forgot Bobby Bear."

"I know," said Liza. "Come on, we'll get him now."

Liza and Daniel ran to the house. Liza shouted, "Gran, Grandpa, they're coming."

Liza and Daniel went inside. The others followed them into the kitchen.

"We had to come," said Mrs. Hawkins. "The waiting was

getting to all of us. I left a message for Jean Marsh to call me here."

"Then you have talked to her," said Grandpa.

"Yes," said Mrs. Hawkins. "She had to check on some things."

"I'm sure everything will turn out well," said Gran. "I have some fresh coffee made."

"That sounds good," said Hermit Dan.

Gran had just poured the coffee when the telephone rang.

"I'm sure that's her," said Mrs. Hawkins, almost running to the telephone.

All eyes were on Mrs. Hawkins, but nobody could tell what was happening. Mrs. Hawkins seemed to be doing a lot of listening and agreeing. Finally they heard her say, "Then it's all set. Thank you!"

Mrs. Hawkins hung up the receiver. Then she surprised everyone. Mrs. Hawkins jumped up and down shouting, "Hurray!"

Hermit Dan stood up. His face was all smiles. He said, "Then the answer is yes!"

"It sure is," said Mrs. Hawkins. She ran to Hermit Dan and hugged him.

Then Mrs. Hawkins said, "Mark, Carrie, Daniel, you have yourselves a grandmother."

"And a grandfather," said Hermit Dan.

"Huh!" said Bill.

"Why not?" asked Hermit Dan. "I live right next door. I promised the social worker I would help Jenny with the children."

Carrie began to cry.

"What's wrong, dear?" asked Mrs. Hawkins.

"We've never had grandparents," said Carrie. She ran and threw her arms around Mrs. Hawkins.

"Well, you have them now," said Hermit Dan, picking up Daniel. Then he noticed Mark. He asked, "What's wrong, son?"

"I can't believe it," said Mark. "It seems too good to be true."

"Hey," said Bill, "you mean they're going to live on Pirate Island with you?"

"That's right," said Mrs. Hawkins.

"You mean they won't have to go to school?" asked Bill. "That's not fair."

"Of course they will go to school," said Hermit Dan. "That's one of the things Ms. Marsh was checking on. A boat will take them to Mainland and bring them back every day."

"We won't even have to change schools," said Carrie. "I'll have my same friends."

"Going to school by boat sounds like fun," said Jed. "Would you like a few more foster grandchildren?"

"We'll volunteer," said Liza.

Everybody laughed and began to make jokes. Finally Mrs.

Hawkins said, "All right, children, let's go home. We have a lot of planning to do."

"I'm glad me and my kitten have the same home," said Daniel.

"Hey, how about us?" said Mark. "Aren't you glad we all have the same home?"

"I knew we would," said Daniel. "I didn't know where my kitten was."

After everybody left, Liza, Bill, and Jed sat at the table with their grandparents. Gran looked at Liza and said, "Why the tears?"

"That was the happiest ending to a mystery I ever saw," said Liza.

"So she cries," said Bill. "What would have happened with a sad ending?"

"I don't know," answered someone. "What would have happened?"

"Dad!" shouted the children.

"I'm here too," said another voice.

"Mom!" shouted the children.

"What a day filled with surprises," said Gran. She hugged her son and his wife.

"I take it these three haven't driven you mad," said Mom.

"Who, us?" said the children.

"Unless there are some ghosts around I can't see," said Dad.

"Ghosts!" said Jed, "the magic word."

"Nice friendly ghosts," said Liza. "I'll never be afraid of ghosts again."

Mom and Dad looked puzzled. Dad said, "I don't understand."

Everybody laughed as Bill said, "It's a long story."